RAINBOW PLACE

(RAINBOW PLACE #1)

JAY NORTHCOTE

COPYRIGHT

Cover artist: Garrett Leigh.
Editor: Victoria Milne.
Rainbow Place © 2018 Jay Northcote.

ALL RIGHTS RESERVED

This literary work may not be reproduced or transmitted in any form or by any means, including electronic or photographic reproduction, in whole or in part, without express written permission.
This is a work of fiction and any resemblance to persons, living or dead, or business establishments, events or locales is coincidental.
The Licensed Art Material is being used for illustrative purposes only. All Rights Are Reserved. No part of this may be used or reproduced in any manner whatsoever without written permission, except in the case of brief quotations embodied in critical articles and reviews.

Warning

This book contains material that is intended for a mature, adult audience. It contains graphic language, explicit sexual content, and adult situations.

ONE

"It's just so depressing sometimes." Seb sighed and took another gulp of the rather delicious Shiraz in his glass. "It's not that I care about being different. I *like* being different. But it's lonely as hell feeling like I'm the only gay in a fifty-mile radius, because all the others are underage or in the closet—or both."

"The only gay in the village?" Penny snorted. "Yeah, we know that feeling. There aren't too many out lesbians around either."

"And try being a black lesbian," Trude said, lips quirking in a smile. "I'm rarer than hen's teeth in this part of the world."

"But honestly, sweetie. What were you expecting when you moved here?" Penny asked. "You must have known what it would be like out here in the sticks."

"Yeah." Seb took another swig, draining his glass, which was immediately topped up by Trude. "It's not that it's a surprise, exactly. It's more that the reality bothers me more than I expected it would."

When Seb had taken the bold move to leave London

and relocate to a seaside town in Cornwall, he had known it would be a very different life. But he hadn't anticipated how hard it would be to be cut off from the diversity of the city. He missed the gay bars, queer bookshops, and other LGBT-friendly spaces. At thirty-six years old, bruised from yet another relationship break-up, he'd been ready for a change of direction. With nothing to tie him to London anymore, the opportunity to live by the sea had lured him in. But four weeks on, it felt nothing like home, and sometimes Seb wondered if he'd made a terrible mistake. If it wasn't for Penny and Trude taking him under their gloriously queer wings, he'd probably have slunk back to London with his tail between his legs by now.

It was pure luck that he'd ended up renting a house next door to the only out queer couple in the town. They'd met in the first week when Seb had accidentally rolled his VW Golf into Penny's Mini after a messed-up hill start. He'd turned up with his insurance details and a bottle of wine to apologise. Three bottles of wine later they were his new best friends, as well as his accountant (Penny) and webdesigner (Trude).

Penny and Trude lived together openly as a married couple, with Trude's fourteen-year-old son, Carson, and seemed accepted by the local community. But Seb was yet to find other out gay men in Porthladock.

"Maybe you should try a hook-up app?" Penny suggested. "That would be the best way of finding other gay men, surely?"

"Been there, done that, deleted it," Seb said glumly. "There was nobody who caught my eye. Too many blank profiles, and all the guys close to my age were claiming to be discreet—which either means married to a woman, or in the closet, or both. There were more younger guys, but I'm not interested in under thirties." Any reasonably attractive guys under thirty were way too critical in Seb's experience.

"I'm sorry." Penny took Seb's free hand and squeezed.

"It's not the end of the world. I'm happy being single—for a while anyway—but it would be nice to make some more gay friends. Thank God for you two." Seb smiled at Penny. "But I miss feeling part of a queer community. It's sad that there's no focus for LGBT people down here. No support groups, no pub nights, no clubs. Nothing."

"Maybe you should start something." Trude eyed him over her glass, eyebrows raised in a challenge.

"I should make the café gay." Seb grinned. "I could queer it up and serve rainbow cake, and decorate it with glittery paint."

Seb's new business venture was a café/bar. It was something he'd always dreamed of doing. He'd managed to find the perfect premises and had just received planning permission for change of use, so he was ready to start renovating with a view to opening in a couple of months.

Penny laughed, but Trude said seriously, "You should."

They both turned to look at her.

"I was kidding!" Seb said.

"I know you were, but I don't think it's such a bad idea. You're right that this town has nothing for queer people, and even if most of them are invisible they're still here. Statistically there must be lots of others living here. Making a place that's LGBT-friendly might help to bring people together, form that community you're missing."

"Yeah, but they're invisible because they're in the closet." Seb frowned. "So they're hardly going to come rushing out to eat rainbow cake when I open the place. A gay café would be business suicide here. I'd be bankrupt in a month."

Trude shrugged. "I wouldn't be so sure. Sometimes people are only invisible because they don't have a reason to be visible. If you give people a safe place to be themselves, they'll come. You don't have to make it super gay, just gay-friendly. Then that doesn't exclude non-queer people. But it would give you a unique selling point because there's nothing like that down here. I think if you pitched it exactly right it could work."

"There are locals who would support it," Penny said thoughtfully. "Especially the younger generation; the sixth formers from Porthladock High might like the idea."

"Yes!" Trude said, clapping her hands. "Carson tells me there are kids at his school who are out as gay, bi, queer, trans. Those kids would come and would bring their friends. And you'd get a lot of your trade from tourists too remember. Plus people would come from further afield if you had events to draw them in. You could have bands in the evening, or karaoke. You could even have a drag show."

Seb felt a swell of excitement in his chest, like a wave just before it breaks. "I love the idea," he admitted. "But do you really think it could work?"

"I think it's possible," Penny said. "Cornwall might be traditional in some ways, but we also have lots of unusual people. Artists, musicians, people into communal living or other alternative lifestyles. Places that offer something a little different can do well here if they hit the right note. People like quirky, and they like something original. I think it might be worth the risk. If you need help in how to promote it, then look no further." She gestured at Trude. "We have a PR wizard right here."

"I think wizard is a little strong," Trude said. "PR isn't my speciality."

"Oh come, you're great at promotion as well as the web

side of things. You know loads about social media and how to target advertising."

"Sounds brilliant." Seb beamed at them both. "I love the concept, so I'll definitely consider it."

AFTER SLEEPING ON THE IDEA, Seb woke early the next morning with his brain whirling with possibilities.

He was due to meet with a potential contractor today about the renovation, and was full of energy and excitement at the prospect of finally getting started with the practical side of the business. As he ate breakfast and drank his morning coffee, Seb went over the suggestions from last night and made a list of the ideas they'd come up with, adding a few more of his own in the process. He loved the idea of making the café/bar a queer-friendly space. Part of him doubted whether it was viable, but despite his reservations he desperately wanted to try.

IT WAS A BEAUTIFUL SPRING MORNING. As Seb walked down the steep, narrow streets to the centre of town, the sun was out in a gloriously blue sky, and the usual noisy seagulls circled overhead. He caught glimpses of the sea between the houses, and deliberately took a slightly longer route so he could walk along the harbour. The water always called to him, and he couldn't resist the urge to stop and admire the view for a few minutes.

Leaning on the railing, Seb looked out at the natural harbour created where the river joined the sea. Hundreds of boats were moored; all shapes and sizes bobbing gently on the water. A few sailors were already out; little dinghies zipping back and forth near the sailing club, and larger vessels heading out to sea. With the sun warm on his face, Seb was filled with a rush of happiness. For all his complaining last night, he wouldn't trade this for all the gay clubs in London. Settling in somewhere new and finding your tribe took time, and Seb was prepared to be patient.

He checked the time on his phone, and reluctantly tore himself away from the seafront to make his way back to the high street that ran parallel to the water, lined with buildings on either side. The pavement was too narrow to be much use, and pedestrians were blocking the road as cars and delivery drivers struggled to get through. Seb joined the chaos, now practised at ducking into shop doorways or squeezing up against the wall as vehicles passed at a snail's pace.

The place Seb had found to rent was in a great location. About halfway along the high street, it used to be a greengrocers and was flanked by a clothes shop on one side and a bakery on the other. Opposite was a gallery selling work by local artists. Seb paused outside to look at the exterior. It was nothing much to look at now, just the front door with a large window either side. But Seb could imagine how it would look when it was open. He'd have a brightly coloured sign over the door, and was going to have two tables right by the windows for customers who like people watching. A menu displayed outside would help to encourage people through the doors, or so he hoped.

Unlocking the door, Seb stepped inside and let his imagination keep flowing. Lighting would be key, given that the only natural light came from the front windows. He wanted it bright enough in the day so it wouldn't feel gloomy, but with the option of making it more subtle in the evening to give an intimate feel. He'd have flowers on all the tables, and candles in the evening. Closing his eyes, he could almost hear the chatter of customers and smell the food from the kitchen.

"Um, excuse me. Are you Mr Radcliffe?"

Pulled out of his daydream, Seb opened his eyes to the dirty, dust-covered interior. Huge cobwebs hung from the exposed beams and an unpleasant smell of damp permeated the space. They had a long way to go, but with planning permission granted, there was nothing to stop him now.

"Yes, hi." Seb turned and held out a hand to greet the tall man standing awkwardly behind him on the narrow strip of pavement. "You must be Mr Dunn."

"Jason, please." He took Seb's hand in a powerful grip.

"Hello, Jason. And please call me Seb." Seb gave him a quick once over, noticing immediately how attractive Jason was. Easily over six foot and broad with it, he was powerfully built. Chiselled features were softened by a short beard that glinted gold in the sunlight, and his eyes were the dark greyish blue of the sea. His mid-brown hair was thick and wavy, and made Seb want to run his hands through it to see if it felt as good as it looked. His smile was nervous and he didn't hold Seb's gaze for long. Seb released Jason's hand, noticing the brush of his calloused palm as he did so.

A car horn blared, making them both jump.

"Shit, sorry. Come in." Seb stood aside so Jason could step in out of the path of the van driver who was glaring at him. "Mind your head."

Jason ducked just in time to avoid the low doorframe of the inner door that led from the porch into the main room, and Seb made a mental note to put a clear sign and some hazard tape on that for taller customers. At five-foot-eight, Seb fitted easily underneath it with inches to spare.

"So, on the phone you mentioned that you're looking to convert this space into a café, is that correct?" Jason looked around the interior carefully, a small furrow of concentration between his brows.

"Yes. Well, actually now I'm considering going the whole hog and making it a café/bar. I've been given planning permission to change it to licensed premises, and that means I can open later and attract different customers in the evening."

"Okay," Jason said thoughtfully, walking ahead of Seb towards the back of the main room where it was dark and gloomy. Seb probably should have put the lights on, but they were ugly strip lights and it was easier for him to imagine the potential of the place in the dim light from the window at the front. "You've got a lot of space to work with. That's good."

"Yes." Seb followed him, excitement building again at Jason's obvious interest in the project. "It's much bigger on the inside than you'd expect from the facade. And there's an extension on the back, which is where I want the kitchen, so the whole of this room can be used for seating apart from one corner for the bar."

"Can I see the space where you want the kitchen?"

"Of course. This way." Seb passed Jason, leading him to a door at the back. It opened with a creak into darkness. The blinds were down over the window of the extension, and Seb reached for the light switch in the gloom. But when he flipped it, there was a brief flash of light and then nothing. "Bollocks," he said. "The bulb blew. Hang on; let me get the blinds up." Carefully, Seb picked his way through the room. He could just make out the strips of pale light filtering around the edges of the blinds, but the back room was full of stuff. Furniture he'd picked up in junk shops that he thought might be useful, and crap left behind by the previous tenants that he hadn't got rid of yet. "Ouch!" he yelped as he hit his shin on something hard and stumbled, falling forward, arms flailing. His hands landed on a flat and mercifully stable surface, catching him before he face-planted into the unknown.

"Are you okay?" Jason's voice was concerned.

"Yes, yes. I'm fine." Heart pounding, Seb paused for a moment, leaning over the low table he seemed to have landed on, relieved not to have made a total tit of himself in front of Jason.

A light flashed on, illuminating the space, and Seb realised Jason was using his phone as a torch. "Clever." He gave a self-deprecating chuckle. "I should have thought of that, shouldn't I?"

"Are you sure you're okay?" Jason's voice was close behind him now, and Seb realised he was in a rather compromising position with his hands on a coffee table and his arse in the air. Normally he'd have been happy to bend over for a guy like Jason, but not unless he thought Jason was into the idea too.

Straightening up quickly, Seb brushed himself down, and turned to find Jason standing much closer than he expected. "Oh!" He took a step back and hit his legs on the table again and nearly fell backwards this time. A strong hand grabbed his elbow, keeping him upright. "Thanks. God, I'm not usually so clumsy." Seb's cheeks were burning with embarrassment. If only Jason wasn't so attractive this would be way less awkward. "You can let go of me now. I promise I won't fall over again."

Jason snatched his hand away as if Seb was on fire and took a step back. "Sorry."

"It's fine. Now let me get those blinds up." Seb hurried to the window and pulled on the cord. The blinds were stiff, which was why he'd left them shut, but he managed to open them and fasten the cord. "I should tear these down. They need replacing anyway." He turned in time to see Jason look up quickly, a guilty flush on his cheeks.

Was he staring at my arse?

Surely Seb must be mistaken. He hadn't got a gay vibe from Jason, but then he hadn't been looking for it, so maybe…? But no. He shook himself, trying to get his brain back onto business and away from stupid daydreams about the hot builder. Any interest he thought he'd seen must have been wishful thinking on his part. "So, this is going to be the kitchen." He gestured around the cluttered space. "I'm thinking a central island for prep, cookers against that wall, fridges and freezers there, sinks under the window—where there's already plumbing—and storage cupboards on all the remaining wall space. What do you reckon?"

TWO

Jason desperately tried to haul his mind back onto the job as Seb stared at him expectantly.

Seb was distractingly cute, and clearly gay from the way he kept looking at Jason as though he was edible. He didn't have a problem with Seb's sexuality—it would be hypocritical if he did—but Jason was deep in the closet and very comfortable there, thank you very much. Living in a small town, and working in an industry where men tended to be very masculine, Jason didn't like people knowing his business. He kept his private life very private, which meant the occasional hook-up with other discreet locals or visitors to the area, and he had no plans to change that.

Working closely with Seb would be challenging when Jason found him so attractive. But Jason badly needed this job. Money had been tight recently, and this was going to be a big project. Jason had to impress Seb so he could secure the contract.

Pulling a notepad and pen out of his back pocket, Jason nodded in a way he hoped looked thoughtful as he tried to stop thinking about the curve of Seb's arse and focus on the matter in hand.

"That all sounds good. What materials do you want for the surfaces?"

"Stainless steel."

"And do you want gas or electric cookers?"

Feeling more in control of the situation now, Jason relaxed and made notes as Seb explained his plans in more detail, prompted by the occasional question from Jason.

When they were finished in the kitchen they went back to the main room and Seb went through his vision for the layout. It all sounded manageable. Jason and his assistant, Will, would handle the building side of things along with plastering and decorating. He'd need to contract in plumbers to sort out the kitchen and put in a new toilet to replace the grotty old one, but he had the skills to do the electrics himself.

"That all sounds manageable in the timescale you want," Jason said, putting his notepad away. "I'll need to do some calculations and then I'll get back to you with a quote as soon as possible."

"Brilliant." Seb beamed and it was like the sun coming out. Clapping his hands, Seb spun around. "I can't wait to make my plans a reality."

His excitement was infectious and Jason couldn't help but smile back. Seb held his gaze, and the atmosphere was charged as Jason stared, finally allowing himself to take in Seb's appearance. He'd mainly noticed his arse before but hadn't appreciated the whole package.

Damn. He's exactly my type.

Shorter than Jason, and slim, Seb was too old to be called a twink, but he was still attractive in a boyish way despite the fact that he must be well into his thirties. His hair was dark and styled into a quiff at the front. Clean-shaven with sharp features, and brown eyes Jason could get lost in, he was undeniably gorgeous.

Realising he was still staring at Seb like an idiot, Jason cleared his throat, and turned his attention back to the notepad in his hand. "Right then." He squiggled something unintelligible on the paper to give himself something to do. "I guess I'd better leave you to it. I'll be in touch soon." Finally dragging his gaze back to Seb's face, he found that Seb was watching him. His lips were still curved in a half-smile that was a little too knowing for Jason's comfort.

His heartrate ratcheted up a few notches.

Seb was giving him a look Jason recognised from the rare times he'd travelled to Plymouth or Exeter for a night out in a gay bar or club. It was the look that signalled interest and intent, and normally Jason would have responded to it by smiling back or approaching. But this was too close to home.

He stuck out his hand. "It was a pleasure meeting you."

Seb paused for a fraction before taking Jason's hand. "You too." His grip was smooth and cool, the pressure light. He brushed his thumb over the palm of Jason's hand as he released him. "I'll look forward to hearing from you. I hope the price is right, because I'd really like to work with you. You came highly recommended." He sounded sincere.

Surprised and pleased, Jason said, "Really? Well that's good to know. Thanks." He put his notepad and pen away and walked to the door. "Bye then." He just remembered to duck his head in time as he passed through the inner door.

"Bye," Seb called after him.

In the street, the sun was bright. Jason took a deep breath of the sea air and blinked, letting his eyes adjust. Out here in the sunshine and bustle of the high street of Porthladock, it was like he'd stepped into a different world after the dim interior of Seb's soon-to-be café.

Crossing the street, Jason turned and put his hands in his pockets, studying the building from the outside. It was easy to imagine it with a new sign outside, tables in the window, customers coming and going.

Normally Jason would be thrilled at the prospect of a job that would not only be lucrative but also an enjoyable project. Hearing about Seb's plans had inspired him. Jason loved working his magic on a space and turning it into something new, and the old shop was going to look amazing when the conversion was complete. But the idea of working so closely with Seb for the duration left him uneasy. Jason suspected he'd already given himself away. If Seb didn't know Jason swung his way, then he must have an inkling. Gay men usually had a good instinct for that, and Jason hadn't exactly managed to be subtle.

Turning, Jason set off at a brisk walk. He needed to get back to his current job of fixing up a holiday cottage ready for the summer season. Jason had left Will to his own devices while he came to meet Seb, and he wanted to check the lad was getting on okay. He was a good worker, but still inexperienced.

"OH, HI, JASE." Anna gave Jason a quick hug and kiss on the cheek in greeting as she always did. "Come in."

"Hi." Jason took off his heavy work boots before stepping into the house he used to share with Anna before they split up. It still felt odd being invited into the place he'd once called home.

"I'm afraid Zoe's in the shower and still needs to pack. Do you want a cup of tea while you wait?"

"That would be lovely, thanks."

At twelve years old, Zoe was getting to the age where she'd spend ages showering. It didn't help that her hair was thick and wavy—like Jason's—and came halfway down her back. But she was way too independent to accept any help in combing through the tangles after washing it.

Fortunately Jason and Anna got on well, so Jason never minded hanging around waiting for his daughter to be ready when he came to collect her for a night at his place. He took a seat at the kitchen table while Anna made them both some tea.

"Do you want a blueberry muffin? Zoe did some baking yesterday."

"I'd love one, thanks."

Anna joined him at the table with tea and a muffin on a plate for Jason.

"Cheers." Jason smiled at her, and Anna grinned back.

"So, how's life? We haven't had a chance to catch up for a while."

"Not bad thanks. Busy with work, which is good. Just finishing up one job and have the prospect of a new one starting soon. How about you?"

"Great actually. My private practice is really picking up, which means I might drop some of the NHS stuff soon." Anna was a counsellor, and had recently started seeing clients at home around her day job.

"Good for you. And how's your mum? Is she back on her feet after the hip replacement?"

"Yes, she's doing well. She'll be able to start driving again soon, which will be good for her."

"And you too, I imagine." Jason took a sip of his tea.

"Yes. Playing taxi is getting a little tiring."

"You know you can always ask me if you need. I'm happy to help out."

Anna smiled. "Thanks, Jason. That's good to know. But I'm managing. Ben has been pitching in which helps. He took her to her post-op appointment yesterday because I was running an anger management group."

"That's good." Jason ignored the small flash of hurt at her rejection of his help.

"Speaking of Ben...." Anna looked down at the mug in her hands briefly and then met Jason's gaze again. "We've been talking about him moving in here."

"Oh." Jason hadn't seen that coming. Maybe he should've; Anna had been seeing Ben for almost a year now and he stayed over there half the time already. "Right. Okay."

"I hope you feel all right about that? He's really good with Zoe, and I've discussed it with her. She's happy for him to move in soon—once he's given notice on his flat."

"Yes. Of course." Jason wasn't sure he was totally fine with it, but he'd get used to the idea. Ben was a good man, and Jason wanted Anna to be happy. It felt odd imagining another man taking his place in the house he'd done up when he and Anna first married.

"He's not replacing you, Jase," Anna said softly. "You're Zoe's dad and Ben moving in won't change that."

"I know that. It's fine. You deserve happiness, and God knows I wasn't able to give it to you."

"It wasn't all bad."

"But it's better with Ben."

Anna shrugged. "Of course. He's straight, Jase. He's not going through the motions, trying to be someone he's not." Her voice was kind.

Their separation had been relatively painless, and that

was mostly thanks to Anna. She'd been the one to make Jason see what was wrong. He was so deep in denial he hadn't wanted to admit the sexual chemistry just wasn't there between them. He'd always put it down to marrying young. At twenty, Anna was only the second girl he'd slept with and he'd loved her for her personality and sense of humour. When she fell pregnant with Zoe early in their relationship that had seemed like a good enough reason to get married.

"Yeah." Jason stared down at his tea, the old guilt still catching him when he thought about the mistakes he'd made.

After an uncomfortable silence, Anna said brightly, "So, what's this new job you might have lined up?"

Grateful for the subject change, Jason told Anna about the café conversion plans.

"Oh, is that the shop next to Cardew's bakery? It's a nice location for another café. Do you know what sort of menu they'll be offering?"

"I didn't ask. I was only focusing on the building side of things."

"Typical." Anna chuckled. "Whereas I want to know what cake they'll be selling."

"It's going to be a bar as well as a café, so I expect the menu will be different in the evening."

"It sounds exciting. And the guy who's running it, did he seem nice? He's new to the area, yes?"

"Yeah, he's definitely not local. He seemed like a decent bloke." Jason avoided Anna's gaze, running his finger along a groove in the tabletop where Zoe had scratched it with a fork when she was a toddler. "I'm pretty sure he's gay," he added quietly, unable to resist the urge to talk about Seb to the one person who knew his secret.

"Really? What made you think that?"

Jason shrugged. "He had that quality some gay men have. Not all, obviously. But the more camp ones who don't try and hide it." It was hard to describe, something about the tone and lilt of Seb's voice, and the way he moved. "But mostly it was the way he looked at me." Heat unfurled in Jason's belly at the memory of Seb's eyes on him, assessing, approving, wanting. He was sure it hadn't been his imagination.

"Are you interested?" Anna asked, voice carefully casual, but she couldn't hide the spark of excitement in her eyes or the slight smile that tugged at the corners of her mouth.

"In the project, yes," Jason said dryly. "Which is why I need to stay focused on that and not be distracted by the guy who might be hiring me."

"So you *do* like him." Anna grinned.

"But I'm not going to do anything about it." Jason drank the last of his tea and put the mug down. He traced his finger around the rim, the skin snagging on a chip.

"Jason."

He raised his eyes reluctantly to meet Anna's gaze, lifting his eyebrows in question, even though he knew what was coming.

"Why are you so worried about people finding out you're gay?"

"I don't like people knowing my business," Jason replied, knowing that was only a half-truth.

Anna persisted. "Nobody will care that much."

"My dad will."

"He's hardly in your life now. It shouldn't matter what he thinks." Jason's parents had retired to Spain, and only came back to visit a couple of times a year. "And yes, you'll get a few raised eyebrows I'm sure, and some idiots might mutter about it, but so what? It's who you are, there's nothing wrong with it, and wouldn't it be nice not to have to keep hiding?"

Jason stood, chair legs scraping the tiled floor. "It's my life." His voice came out sharper than he'd intended, but Anna had touched a nerve. "I'm going to go and chase up Zoe. I want to get home so I can make tea."

"I'm sorry," Anna said. "I know it's not my business, but I worry about you, Jase. It seems like a lonely way of living to me."

"I'm fine," Jason insisted. "Really, Anna. I'm quite happy as I am."

Was he though? Happiness seemed like something elusive anyway; Jason had never seen the point in chasing it. He just got on with things and kept himself busy. Between his work, his hobbies, and Zoe, he didn't have time for a relationship. Occasional hook-ups scratched his itch for sex and he'd never met a guy he wanted more with. Jason enjoyed his own company and had no desire to share his life with anyone else for now. "I'll go and see if Zoe's nearly ready."

Upstairs, Jason knocked on Zoe's bedroom door. Loud pop music boomed on the other side, so when there was no reply, Jason knocked harder.

"Yeah?" His daughter called over the music.

Assuming it was safe to enter as he hadn't got the usual yell of, "Don't come in!" he got when it wasn't, Jason opened her door and peered around it to see Zoe at her dressing table putting on lip gloss. Her hair was damp and cascaded down her back in tendrils.

"Hi, sweetheart." He grinned when he caught her eye in the mirror. "You nearly ready to go?"

"Hi, Dad." She stopped what she was doing and came over to hug him. "Yeah. I just need to finish my make-up."

Jason resisted the urge to tell her she was beautiful without it.

"Okay." He sat on the edge of her bed. "So how's my favourite girl? Have you had a good week since I saw you last?"

"It's been all right. I've got too much homework though. Will you help me with my maths tonight?"

"Of course."

He watched as Zoe carefully applied mascara to her lashes. Twelve seemed awfully young to be worrying about make-up, but Anna assured him most of Zoe's contemporaries wore it too—although not to school because they'd be sent to wash it off if they did.

Once she was done, she got up and picked up her bag from the bed. "I'm ready. Can we get pizza for dinner tonight?"

"No. I've got pasta to cook. But maybe we can get pizza on Saturday again." He checked his watch. It was already six. Dinner was going to take a while, and by the time he'd helped Zoe with homework it would be late before he was able to sit down and do the quote for Seb. "Come on then. Hurry up and say goodbye to your mum so we can get back to mine."

SURE ENOUGH, Jason was yawning by the time he finally sat down with his battered old laptop once Zoe was in bed. It took him a while to sort out the figures as there was a lot to plan for, and when he was done he double and triple-checked them because his brain was foggy with the need for sleep.

That done, he drafted an email to Seb and attached the quote. Pausing for a moment, he let his finger hover over the trackpad poised to click send. He desperately wanted this job, but he was anxious too. The thought of working in such close proximity to Seb for weeks had his heart racing.

Fuck it. What's the worst that could happen?

He hit send.

THREE

Two weeks later

SEB WAS up bright and early on the day Jason was due to start work on the café. The blue sky and sunshine matched his mood as he walked down the hill into town, anticipation fluttering in his stomach. He tried telling himself that it was all about the project, but deep down he knew he was excited about seeing Jason again too.

The burly builder had been on Seb's mind since their first meeting. Seb had been thrilled when Jason's quote was affordable, and although he was impatient to get started, he hadn't minded waiting for Jason to finish his previous job. A friend of Penny's had recommended Jason as reliable and hardworking, and Seb could be patient for the right person. But now the day had finally come, Seb was full of pent-up excitement. His dream was about to begin its transition into reality, and the guy who'd been starring in his fantasies for the last fortnight was going to be the one to make it happen.

If only Jason could make those *other* wishes come true too.

Seb remembered the flash of interest he'd glimpsed in Jason's eyes on their first meeting. It was hard to be sure if it had been genuine or whether Seb had been mistaken. He'd tried to signal interest back, but either he'd been wrong or Jason wasn't interested because the shutters had come down, and whatever Seb thought he'd seen was gone.

Reaching the soon-to-be café, Seb sighed wistfully as he unlocked the door and let himself in. Standing in the gloomy interior, he let his mind wander for a moment before shaking his head firmly. He turned the lights on, snapping himself back to reality.

Behave.

He needed to keep things professional, and lusting after Jason once they were working together wasn't okay. Maybe Jason wouldn't live up to Seb's memory of him anyway.

That hope was eradicated when Jason came through the door ten minutes later.

He was just as gorgeous as Seb had remembered, even better in fact.

"Morning," Jason said gruffly. "How are you?"

So wide his shoulders nearly filled the doorway, he had to stoop to avoid bumping his head. Seb wanted to climb him like a tree. It was impossible not to imagine that solid, muscular body under his hands, or how good the weight of Jason would feel pinning him to a mattress. As Seb's imagination whirled into overdrive he realised he was frozen, staring like an idiot.

Pulling himself together, Seb hurried forward with an inane smile pasted onto his face. He held out a hand. "Hi, Jason. Great to see you again. I'm good, thanks. You?" His palm was embarrassingly sweaty as they shook.

"Yeah, not bad, cheers." Jason pulled his hand away quickly. "This is Will, my assistant."

It was only then that Seb registered another man who was lurking behind Jason. Hands in his pockets, Will gave Seb an awkward nod. "Alright, mate." He was young, and tough-looking with buzzed dark hair and stubble. Burly like Jason, Will was a little shorter.

"Hi, Will."

Will ducked his head down to look at his feet. Clearly social skills weren't his forte, but as long as he was a good worker that was all Seb cared about.

"You okay for us to crack on then?" Jason asked. "We're going to start by getting rid of all the old junk you don't want. Will's gonna help me move it all to the front of the shop, and then we'll bring my van down and load it up. I'm hoping we can get all that cleared out today."

"Yes, that's fine. I'm meeting with my accountant this morning. She's coming here, so we'll set up a table wherever we'll be least in the way." Seb wanted to be on the premises to make sure Jason didn't accidentally chuck out anything he was planning on keeping.

PENNY ARRIVED HALF AN HOUR LATER, looking scarily efficient in a dark blue trouser suit with her curly red hair piled on top of her head.

"Wow," Seb said. "You look fantastic." Normally Penny dressed casually for their meetings.

"I have an appointment with a big corporate client this afternoon, so I'm in full-on professional mode today to make me feel the part."

"I'm sorry it's a bit dusty." Seb brushed off a chair for her to sit on. He'd moved a table to the side of the room a little back from the windows where Jason and Will were collecting the stuff to take to the dump.

"It's fine." Penny sat and pulled an iPad, notebook, and pen out of her bag.

Seb took a seat too and opened the file he'd already laid out on the table.

The crash of the kitchen door banging open made Penny jump and turn to see Jason struggling through backwards, holding one end of a large cabinet.

"Steady, Will. Take it slow," Jason said.

It was a tight fit. The door swung back on them and Jason cursed as it bumped into his hand.

Seb jumped up and hurried over. "Let me hold that." He grabbed the door handle and held the door out of their way as the two men eased the furniture through the tight space.

"Thanks," Jason said breathlessly. Muscles bulged in his forearms and there were patches of sweat on his grey T-shirt. He flashed Seb a grateful grin and Seb smiled back, hopelessly smitten.

"It's no trouble. Just shout if you need help again."

Will avoided Seb's gaze as he passed him, frowning with the effort. Seb followed them to the front of the shop, feeling useless but not wanting to desert them in case they needed him.

Jason huffed when they finally put it down by the front door. "Blimey, I'm glad there's only one like that to move." He mopped his brow.

"Told you we should have smashed it up," Will said.

"Aren't you going to introduce me, Seb?" Penny asked brightly. She stood and walked over, high heels clacking on the stone floor. "I'm Penny, Seb's accountant. You must be

Jason." She held out her hand. "I've heard lots about you but we've never met."

"Good things I hope," Jason said as he shook.

Seb cringed. Penny had definitely heard way too much about how hot Jason was, because after half a bottle of Shiraz Seb had no verbal filter and had bored her and Trude stupid about his crush.

"Very good things. You have a good reputation." She turned to Will, "And you are?"

Will stared at her with obvious admiration on his face, which slowly turned pink as she looked at him expectantly.

"This is Will," Jason said, amusement quirking his lips as Will appeared struck dumb.

"Hello, Will," Penny said kindly. She didn't offer a hand, maybe sensing that would be too much for Will to cope with.

Jason nudged Will, who finally remembered his manners. "Hi," he said gruffly, finally tearing his gaze away from Penny and looking down at his feet.

Seb felt a flash of sympathy for him. He knew all about how hard it was having to interact with someone you fancied, and poor Will's crush on Penny was as unrequited as his was on Jason. "Come on, Penny. Let's get started on these figures." He led her back to the table, leaving Will to escape. "But do ask me if you need any more help," he called back over his shoulder to Jason. "I may not be much use at lifting heavy stuff, but door-holding I can manage."

"Okay, thanks."

"I can see why you like him," Penny said quietly once Jason and Will were back in the kitchen. "He's very handsome—if you like that sort of thing."

"And I do." Seb sighed. "But shh, because now is not the time for this conversation."

"Sorry." She mimed zipping her lips and opened her iPad cover. "Now, let's have a look at your proposed pricing and profit margins."

AN HOUR later Seb's head was spinning with numbers and he was exhausted from concentrating and trying to keep up with Penny's mathematically superior brain. Having Jason walking back and forth looking all sweaty and masculine while carrying heavy things hadn't really helped him focus.

"Can we take a break?" he begged. "I'm gasping for a coffee."

"Oh yes, I could use a caffeine top-up myself."

"Ironically, I'll have to nip out to the Seaview Café to get some to take away." Seb grinned ruefully. "I still don't have any plumbing, let alone anything to make decent coffee with here." He stood and stretched. "I'll go and see if Jason and Will need anything."

Seb made his way to the kitchen at the back. The door was propped open with a brick now, so as he approached he had a perfect view of Jason crouching to lift a box full of old leather-bound books that Seb had bought from a junk shop in St Austell. Jason's jeans stretched tight over his muscular arse and dipped at the back to show an inch of skin and the barest hint of butt crack.

Trying not to drool, Seb said, "I'm popping out to get some coffee, would either of you like anything?"

Jason turned; holding the box in his arms like it weighed nothing, belying his bulging biceps. "Oh I'd love a cup of tea please."

"Will?" Seb turned to the younger man.

"Yeah, tea for me too."

"Black? White? Sugar?"

"Milk two sugars please," Will replied.

"Just milk for me, thanks. Can I give you some cash for it?" Jason asked.

"No, no. This is on me."

"Okay. Cheers."

"Those books are to stay, by the way, in case you weren't sure." Seb gestured to the box Jason was still holding.

"Oh, right." Jason's eyebrows lifted in surprise. "Glad you told me."

"They're for decoration mainly, although perhaps some customers will want to read them. I just thought they'd look cool on some dark wooden shelves. I want to give the place that cosy feel, so people can imagine they're in someone's living room. You know? That's what I'm aiming for." Seb realised he was rambling. Jason was still stuck holding the box and nodding politely, while Will was looking at Seb as though he was some mysterious creature in a zoo. "So anyway, just stack them somewhere they won't be in your way. I'll go and get the tea. See you in a bit." He hurried away, cursing the verbal diarrhoea that always afflicted him when he was nervous.

"SO WHEN ARE you going to start on the publicity?" Penny asked.

They'd finished going over the financials and were chatting more generally about Seb's plans for the place.

"I'm not quite sure yet. I'm meeting Trude later this week to come up with a plan. I think we want to sit on it until we're closer to being ready, then try and create a bit of a splash in the local press and on social media when we announce the theme of the café."

"So you don't want it to get out before then?"

"No. There's bound to be a bit of negativity, and Trude thinks it's important that we control how the news gets out and have time to prepare for it. She's probably right. I'm sure some of the locals will object to my plans, but hopefully not too many."

"Have you decided on a name yet?"

"No." Seb flipped to a page in his notebook where he'd been jotting down ideas. "I keep thinking of things but nothing feels quite right yet. It's hard coming up with something that suggests queerness without being too obvious." His voice rose and he waved his arms in the air, saying, "If I put a sign over the door that reads 'My Big Fat Gay Café' then I'm going to struggle to get any straight people through the doors, and that's not my intention. I want it to appeal to everyone—apart from homophobic twats. They can fuck off elsewhere." He chuckled, and then started when he heard the tread of boots behind him.

Looking round, Seb saw Jason with a box of rubbish in his arms. Jason caught Seb's eye, but looked away quickly and didn't stop, carrying the box to add to the growing pile by the door.

"Bugger. Do you think he overheard that?" Seb asked quietly when Jason was safely back in the kitchen.

"Maybe," Penny said. "Doesn't he know the theme for the café? I assumed he did, otherwise I'd have reminded you to keep your voice down."

"I didn't mention it. I didn't think it was relevant for the renovation. Do you think he'll care?"

"Why would he? He's just doing a job. But you should probably tell him to keep it to himself until you're ready to make your big announcement."

"Hmm. Yeah. I guess so." Seb frowned, mentally cursing his loud mouth. "I'll talk to him later."

Penny checked her watch. "Okay, sweetie. I need to love you and leave you. I don't want to be late for my afternoon meeting in Truro."

She packed up her things and Seb saw her to the door. "Thanks, Pen. Hope your meeting goes well, and I'll see you soon." He hugged her and kissed her on each cheek.

"Yes, pop over for a drink sometime soon. Friday maybe?"

"Sounds good."

FOUR

Big Fat Gay Café.

The words were still ringing in Jason's ears as he walked up the hill to fetch his van from where he'd parked it that morning. He'd left Will carrying the last smaller bits of junk through. When he got back, they'd be ready to take the first load of rubbish to the dump.

He hadn't heard the whole of Seb and Penny's conversation, but what he had inadvertently eavesdropped on had left him feeling uneasy. What the hell was a 'gay café' anyway? Jason's mind filled with unlikely images of foppish men reading Oscar Wilde over coffee, or waiters dressed in jockstraps serving phallic banana splits. While the second one sounded appealing to Jason on some levels, there was no way that would ever catch on in Porthladock. Surely Seb couldn't be opening a gay café here? Why on earth would he? And if he was, did Jason still want to be involved in this project?

Work was work, and money was money. But with Jason deep in the closet, he baulked at the idea of being part of it. Maybe that was irrational, but it was too close for comfort.

Reaching his van, he got behind the wheel and turned on the engine. It was too late to back out now. That would damage his reputation more than being associated with whatever crazy scheme Seb had planned. Ignoring the anxiety churning in his gut, Jason pulled out of the parking space and headed down the narrow streets to the town centre, tourists ducking into shop doorways to let him pass.

ANNOYINGLY, they couldn't quite manage everything in one load. They packed the van as full as they could, playing *Tetris* with the bits of old furniture and boxes of junk, but there were still a couple of things that wouldn't fit.

When they came back for the second load and had put the stuff in the van, Jason said to Will, "How about you take this up on your own. There's nothing you can't lift without me, and it gives you a chance to get some van-driving practice in while I get started on the plasterwork."

He'd only recently allowed Will to drive the van, particularly around the tricky streets of Porthladock. This would be the first time he'd let Will take it out alone, but the dump was only on the edge of town and it was about time he trusted the lad. This way, Jason could make a start on chipping off the old flaky plaster in the kitchen.

Will's face lit up. "Yeah, awesome."

Jason tossed him the keys. "Drive carefully."

"Sure thing, boss."

Jason walked back into the gloom of the interior. His gaze automatically veered to Seb who was still sitting at the table with papers, notebook, and a laptop spread out in front of him. His usually perfect dark hair was rumpled from his hands and a frown marred his brow. Jason wished he didn't find Seb so fascinating, but he couldn't help his interest.

"You all right?" Jason asked.

Seb looked up in surprise and his frown lifted as he gave Jason a small smile. "Yes, thanks. Just tired and overwhelmed. There's so much to think about."

"Would more coffee help? I owe you a drink." The plaster could wait, and Jason wouldn't mind another cup of tea.

"Oh yes, that would be fantastic. Thanks! But let me pay for them."

"No. I insist. It's my round."

Seb's smile widened. "Okay."

"What do you want?"

"A large skinny vanilla latte with an extra shot of espresso please."

JASON FELT like a right tit ordering Seb's drink. He mumbled the first time so he had to repeat it more loudly, then they asked him if he wanted sugar-free syrup. At least that meant he had the excuse to tell them it wasn't for him.

"Blimey. I dunno. Um... put the normal one in." He hoped that would be okay, but sugar-free stuff often tasted gross.

Ordering his cup of tea was much easier.

When he got back, the front door was standing open and he was able to push the inner door with his foot. Busy concentrating on not spilling the coffee, he cracked his head painfully on the lintel.

"Ouch. Bollocks!" he cursed loudly.

"Oh God, sorry, sorry...." Seb sounded as though it was his fault that Jason was a clumsy twat. He hurried over. "Let me take those." He took the cups from Jason's hands. "Come and sit, let me see your head."

Jason rubbed it. It hurt like a bitch, but his hand came away clean so at least he wasn't bleeding.

Seb's hands were gentle as he explored the bump on Jason's head. "I think it's a good sign when it comes up in a lump. I'm sorry I don't have any ice. Do you want me to see if I can get some? Or I can buy some frozen peas from the Co-op."

"I'm fine," Jason muttered, embarrassed at the fuss. "Honestly. It's nothing."

"You sure?" Seb's face was still close to his. Jason felt the warm brush of his breath on his forehead, and when he inhaled he could smell Seb's cologne, something sweet and citrusy.

"Totally. Now drink your coffee." He slid it across the table. Seb finally stepped back, seemingly satisfied that Jason didn't have brain damage. "Oh.... I didn't know if you wanted sugar-free syrup or not, so I went with the normal one."

"The normal is fine. I do usually have sugar free actually, because I watch my weight"—Seb patted his non-existent belly—"but I don't like it as much, so this will be a treat for me."

"I don't think you need to worry about your weight." Jason let his gaze slide over Seb's torso. He was wearing a jumper in a lightweight fabric that clung to him, showing off his slim body. It didn't look as if he had much spare flesh on him. Jason liked how lean he was. His approval must have shown on his face because when his eyes made it back up to Seb's face, Seb was grinning, one eyebrow raised.

"Like what you see?" His tone was unmistakably flirtatious, the teasing tone only added to the tingle of arousal that was starting to build in the pit of Jason's belly.

Their gazes locked and held, a thread of connection that

was undeniable now. Jason wanted to say yes, to tell Seb he thought he was hot as hell, to reach for him and pull him down onto Jason's lap where his cock was hardening in his jeans....

The creak of the door opening and the heavy tread of Will's boots was a much-needed wake-up call. Heart pounding, Jason turned quickly away from Seb. "Everything all right?"

"Fine," Will said, not seeming to notice the soup of sexual tension he'd waded into. He pulled the van keys out of his pocket and tossed them to Jason who caught them deftly.

Jason stood, picking up his tea. "I'd better get back to work," he said shortly, avoiding Seb's eyes. He was already kicking himself for letting his guard down. There was no way Seb could have missed his interest that time. He'd been too blatant, too careless. But Seb seemed to have that effect on him. Jason needed to rein himself in or this could get out of hand fast.

"Actually, can I keep you for a moment? There was something else I needed to talk to you about." Seb's tone was serious, taking Jason by surprise. Was it a ruse to get Jason alone again? He looked at Seb but his shuttered expression gave no clue to his motives.

"Uh, of course. Will, can you get started on the plaster in the kitchen?"

"Sure." Will didn't comment on the fact that Jason was supposed to have been doing that while he was out.

Once Will had gone and they could hear him hammering the old plaster in the kitchen, Seb said, "It's about my plans for the café. I thought maybe you overheard Penny and me talking earlier, and I'm trying to keep it a secret until I'm ready to start on the official publicity."

He was still standing, and he squared his shoulders as he spoke, as though in challenge.

Jason's heart kicked up a notch. "Yeah, I did hear something. It's not my business though. I'm just here to do my job."

"Of course, but I wanted you to know that it's a secret for now, so not to let anything slip."

"I didn't really catch all the details anyway. What exactly *are* your plans?"

"Have a seat." Seb gestured to the other chair as he sat down. He took the lid off his coffee and had a sip. "God that's divine. I can practically feel the sugar spreading through my bloodstream already. I'd better not let this become a habit otherwise it will be way too much of a temptation once I have my own coffee machine on the premises. I'll be a sugar addict in no time." He gave a nervous chuckle. Jason waited expectantly, hoping his silence would prompt Seb to get back to the point. "So, anyway. The idea is that the café is going to be gay-friendly... well, LGBT-friendly of course. I know it might seem like an odd decision but I really want to give it a try."

He fixed his brown eyes on Jason and his expression was earnest, pleading almost as though he wanted Jason's approval. "You probably guessed I'm gay. I don't exactly hide my light under a bushel in that regard. And moving to Porthladock from London, well, it's a bit of a shock to feel so cut off from any sort of queer community. It made me think of what it must be like for queer people down here, especially the younger ones growing up with no easy way of connecting with people like themselves. I wanted to try to see if I can create something that will encourage that."

"But do you think it's financially viable?" Jason frowned. "I can't see people rushing here to support it, even if they are gay, or LGBT—whatever letter fits." He shied away from using the word "queer." It still felt like an insult, because he remembered how his father used to use the word, scathingly directed at camp actors on television when Jason was young.

"Well, that's the challenge. I don't want to make it so gay that straight people are afraid to come here. I need to be subtle about it. Queer-friendly is the goal, not completely flaming." Seb gave a small grin. "I just want people to know this is a safe place for LGBT people and their friends to hang out, but not to exclude anyone. In most ways it will be like any other café or bar, but the ethos will be inclusivity. We'll publicise it that way, and maybe look at booking evening entertainment with a queer slant: bands, poetry slams, a drag show. We could run a book group for queer fiction. There are so many possibilities." Animated now, Seb's brown eyes shone with enthusiasm, and it was infectious despite Jason's doubts.

An unexpected surge of excitement rushed through Jason, and hope that Seb could make this work, because it would have been easier for Jason growing up here if there had been something like this for him. Something that showed him there was more than one way to be, that being different didn't have to be a bad thing. It was too late for Jason, but maybe for the next generation....

But Jason shook his head. "I don't know. It's certainly different, but you'll be fighting an uphill battle. I don't know many people down here who are open about their sexuality if they're anything other than straight. And people who are in the closet are likely to avoid this place like the plague for fear of what people might think." His heart thumped hard as he spoke.

Seb was silent for a moment. The pause for thought was

disconcerting after his rapid-fire chatter of before. He held Jason's gaze and his expression was one of sympathy. It shot Jason right in the guts with a lurch of discomfort because Jason never allowed himself to admit that being discreet was a bad thing. It was his choice and he was happy with it—wasn't he?

Finally Seb said cautiously, "But maybe that's exactly what some of the closeted people need. Having this place isn't going to force anyone out who doesn't want to be open, but it might let people see that they have options they haven't considered before. They don't need to come through the doors. Just knowing there's somewhere that welcomes queer people, where other LGBT people go to relax and have fun could make a difference."

Jason swallowed on a lump that had formed in his throat. "I suppose," he managed gruffly.

Another awkward silence.

"Jason," Seb said, and then paused as though searching for the right words. "If working for me puts you in a difficult position... I'd understand if you needed to pull out. I don't want you to," he added quickly. "I'd rather you stayed on board, but it has to be your decision."

Jason met his gaze, the seconds ticking away as he battled internally. His instincts were telling him to escape. Cut his losses and get out before things got messy when word got out about Seb's plans—because Jason knew there would be some opposition to it. And maybe he should take the chance to get the hell away from Seb.

Seb who threatened Jason's carefully compartmentalised existence with his flirting and his unashamed openness.

Seb who Jason couldn't help wanting even though he knew he couldn't—*shouldn't*—go there.

Seb who was currently waiting, biting his lip, and looking worried while Jason considered his course of action.

Seb who was brave and honest, and who was trying to do a good thing.

Seb who'd need all the support he could get when the shit hit the fan and the local bigots got wind of his project.

"I'm in," Jason said simply.

Seb's features softened into a smile that made Jason's stomach flip. "Yes?"

"Yeah. I think you're crazy, and I'm not sure whether you can make this work, but I respect the fact that you're doing it. So I'm sticking with it. My private life is my business and doesn't need to come into this." Jason's cheeks heated. That was the closest he'd come to admitting his sexuality to Seb.

"Exactly. Me hiring you doesn't make you gay. Contrary to the beliefs of some, homosexuality isn't actually catching." Seb chuckled.

Driven by a compulsion to finally say it aloud to someone other than Anna, Jason blurted, "Yeah. I was gay before I met you." His heart surged, pounding against his ribs. Relief and elation warred with panic at making himself so vulnerable.

Seb reached across the table and covered Jason's hand with his. "Does anyone else know?"

"My ex-wife." Jason's lips quirked before he added, "And there's a few blokes I met on Fab Guys who probably have an inkling."

Seb burst out laughing. "Yeah. I'd say so."

Jason laughed too, and the tension wrapping tight around him released and he could breathe again.

"Your secret is safe with me." Seth squeezed his hand and then released it.

Jason missed the contact as soon as it was gone. Not wanting the conversation to be over, but unable to think how to prolong it, he picked up his tea. "I suppose I'd better get back there and see how Will's getting on." The hammering in the back room was a reminder that he was slacking. Standing, Jason added, "And your secret is safe with me too. If word gets out about your Big Gay Café before you're ready, it won't be from me."

FIVE

Seb paused and looked up at the sky as he stepped out of the bakery. The early May sun shone on his face. A few clouds still broke up the vivid blue, but after a week of rain it was lovely to have the sunshine back.

A mouthwatering scent drifted up his nose from the bag of pasties he was holding and reminded him of his mission. It was Friday, and the end of Jason and Will's second week of working on the renovation and Seb was treating them to lunch. Full of good intentions to get a healthier sandwich for himself from the deli a little further down the road, he'd been derailed when he'd stepped inside Cardew's and smelt the Cornish pasties—of course here in Cornwall they just called them pasties. Seb rarely let himself eat them because they were loaded with fat and carbohydrates, but they had proved irresistible.

Entering the café, Seb called out, "I'm back. Lunch is here." He took the pasties to the table that he used, and tidied his workspace to make room for them to eat.

Seb had taken to working here during the day rather than at home alone. He enjoyed being on the premises with

Jason and Will, plus he was available to answer any questions Jason might have. If he was honest with himself, he mainly liked being around Jason. Nothing had happened between them since the day when Will had interrupted Seb's flirting. Sometimes Seb caught Jason watching him, and sometimes Jason caught Seb out the same way. The sexual tension between them was obvious, but unacknowledged. Part of Seb longed to force the issue, but he sensed that Jason needed to be the one to take the next step. If Seb was too pushy he'd only make Jason retreat.

Will led the way through the kitchen door with Jason following behind. They joined Seb at the table.

"Here you go, two large pasties." Seb slid the warm paper bags across to them, plus a couple of paper napkins each.

"Cheers," Will said with a brief grin before opening the bag and biting into the pastry.

"You're welcome." Seb was used to Will's quietness now so was able to resist the urge to overcompensate by chatting too much.

"Thanks, Seb. I'm starving." Jason tucked in too, taking a huge bite that made flaky crumbs of pastry shower onto the tabletop.

"I wasn't going to indulge, but I couldn't help myself." Seb rolled his paper bag down, mouth watering. "You're a bad influence. I only got a medium one though."

"Lightweight," Jason teased.

"And trying to stay that way." Seb finally allowed himself a taste and was immediately launched into salty, meaty, carbs heaven. "Oh my God, that's amazing," he mumbled with his mouth still half-full.

Jason grinned at him. "There's a reason Cornwall is famous for these."

"Mmm." Seb took another bite.

Will demolished his lunch in record time. Wiping his mouth with the back of his hand he stood. "I'm going out to get a Coke and some fags. Anyone want anything?"

Seb shook his head, chewing his last mouthful.

"No thanks," Jason said.

Seb licked his greasy fingers as clean as he could get them. Concentrating on that, he didn't notice he was being watched until he looked up—one finger still in his mouth—and caught Jason's gaze. Seb's heart surged at the intense focus there. He wasn't even trying to be sexy, but had inadvertently caught Jason's attention. Making the most of it now he had it, Seb sucked on his finger and then let it slowly slip from between his lips. He smiled. "That was delicious."

Jason flushed and looked away. "Yeah. Cardew's do the best pasties in Porthladock." He scrumpled up his paper bag. "So, did you have a productive morning?"

"Yes, it was good thanks. I was researching food suppliers and have found some I want to work with. I'll be investigating some drinks suppliers this afternoon. Need to make a few calls." Seb leaned back in his chair. He was uncomfortably full now, but resisted the urge to pat his stomach. He didn't want to draw attention to it. "How about you?"

"Yeah, we made a good start on fitting the units in the kitchen. Reckon we'll be nearly done with them by the end of today."

"So all on schedule then?"

"Yes. All going fine so far."

"You still think it will be all ready for me to launch by the twenty-sixth of May as planned?"

"Yes. I'm planning to have everything finished a few

days before that. I'm allowing that extra wiggle room in case of any delays."

A frisson of excitement and nerves rippled through Seb. Opening day was less than four weeks away. Soon his dream was going to become a reality. "Perfect. I'm meeting Trude soon to go through the PR plan. I think we'll be sending out the initial press release shortly after that."

"Exciting times," Jason said. "You ready to cause a stir?"

"I sure am." Seb grinned. "I'm okay with being the centre of attention, and you know what they say: there's no such thing as bad publicity."

Jason snorted. "Hmm. We'll see. Right. I'm going to get back to work." He stood.

"You not taking a lunch break today?" Seb asked, disappointed. Normally Jason took at least half an hour for a sit down and a cup of tea.

"No. I was hoping to get off early today—if that's okay? I've got my daughter coming to mine for the weekend and I want to get to the supermarket before I pick her up from her mum's."

"That's fine. I didn't know you had a kid. How old is she?"

"Twelve going on fifteen." Jason chuckled. "They grow up too fast. Her name's Zoe." He pulled his phone out of his pocket and scrolled, and then held it out to show Seb a photo of a sweet-looking girl with thick wavy blonde hair.

Seb studied it. He could see Jason in the shape of her eyes and nose. "She's gorgeous; she has hair like a mermaid."

"Thanks." Jason's voice was fond, and pride blazed in his eyes. Seb's mental image of Jason realigned a little with this new information. He hadn't imagined Jason as a father. Seb felt a rush of envy. He would have loved to have had a child, but had never been in a relationship with another guy who was interested in being a parent. None of his relationships had been stable or long-term enough for them to consider it anyway, even if they had both been interested.

"Okay, back to the grindstone." Jason put his phone away and took himself off to the kitchen.

Seb watched his retreating form. Broad shoulders, slim hips, and an arse Seb wanted to squeeze. He kept hoping his crush on Jason would abate, but it only seemed to get stronger with every passing day.

WILL WAS the first to leave that afternoon. He passed Seb with a nod. "Have a good weekend," Seb called after him.

"Cheers." The door banged and he was gone.

Checking the time, Seb was surprised to see that it was only three o'clock. Will normally worked till five like Jason. Ready for a break from poring over drink prices online, Seb stood and stretched, and then went into the kitchen.

"Will left early today," he remarked.

"Dentist," Jason said, his back to Seb, head and shoulders lost in a low-level unit where he was busy doing something Seb couldn't see.

"Wow, it's looking good in here." Since Seb had last looked this morning, they'd got all the units fixed to the wall. With the central island also in position, it was finally beginning to look like the kitchen Seb had been imagining when he rented the place.

"Yeah?" Jason crawled out backwards while Seb admired his arse. If only Seb had been paying more attention he might have had time to warn Jason, but as it was it was too late. As Jason straightened up he caught his head on the cupboard door of the unit above, which was hanging open. "Ouch!" Jason flinched and crouched down, hands clutching his head.

"Fuck, are you okay?" Seb rushed over. He knelt beside Jason and gently prised his fingers away. "Let me see. Oh, that looks nasty." Blood was oozing from a small wound just below Jason's hairline. "Come and sit down and I'll get the first aid kit." Seb had invested in a basic kit after Will had cut his thumb a few days ago and Seb had had to run to the chemists to buy plasters. He helped Jason up, and guided him through to a chair in the main room. There was still a napkin on the table from lunchtime. "Hold that on it."

Seb got out the first aid kit and selected an antiseptic wipe. Feeling very efficient, he tore open the wipe and tilted Jason's head up so he could see it properly. "Let me clean it for you."

"I can do it."

"You can't see, and there isn't a mirror here. Let me at it."

Jason obediently moved the napkin out of the way and let Seb dab gently at the cut. He flinched and hissed.

"Does it hurt?"

"Stings a bit," Jason admitted.

"Sorry."

"It's not your fault I'm a clumsy oaf. Although I seem to be even more accident-prone than usual around you."

"You're not the only clumsy one." Seb paused in his ministrations and was glad to see that the bleeding seemed to be slowing down. "Remember me falling over the first day we met?"

"How could I forget? Face down arse up over a coffee table. You made quite an impression." Jason's expression was teasing, a grin tugging at his lips.

"Well that's good to know." Seb dabbed at the cut again.

"Let me get a plaster for that. I think it's stopped bleeding but it's dusty in here and a plaster will keep it clean."

He got a plaster from the first aid kit and leaned over Jason again to carefully stick it over the cut.

"Sorry, I just noticed I stink," Jason said, sniffing his own armpit. "It's been hot work today." His T-shirt had damp patches of sweat on it.

Seb inhaled automatically, and yes, objectively Jason did smell pretty strongly of sweat. But it wasn't unpleasant—far from it. He smelt of hardworking man, of workouts and locker rooms, of all Seb's jock and blue-collar fantasies rolled into one. And fuck; now Seb was getting hard and the lightweight chinos he was wearing wouldn't do a good job of hiding it. But Jason had started flirting first, that mention of Seb's arse was a pretty clear signal.

Throwing caution to the wind, Seb sniffed again, obviously this time, and deliberately let his voice come out a little husky as he straightened up and held Jason's gaze. "You smell pretty great to me." He canted his hips forward slightly, enough so Jason couldn't miss the bulge of Seb's erection given that he was practically eye-level with it.

Sure enough, Jason's gaze dropped to Seb's crotch and fixed there. His pupils spread wide and his lips parted.

Please make a move. Please. Seb waited, his heart beating a frantic rhythm.

"Seb." Jason lifted his hands and then hesitated. He looked up at Seb's face again and Seb could see how conflicted he was. Fear and uncertainty warred with want.

"Do it," Seb said. "Touch me." He moved a tiny bit closer in invitation.

Jason put his hands on Seb's hips, a tentative touch at first, but then his grip tightened and he tugged Seb towards him as he pushed his chair back to make room for Seb on his lap.

Going willingly, Seb tangled his hands in the thick waves of Jason's hair as their mouths met in a kiss. All Jason's hesitance vanished with the contact. He kissed Seb like he was starving for it, a desperate groan escaping. Sliding his hands around to Seb's arse, Jason squeezed, and it was Seb's turn to groan as he pressed down against the bulge of Jason's cock and rubbed his own against Jason's stomach. Everything was rushed and desperate: hands clutching, tongues sliding, teeth clashing.

Lost in the heat of it, Seb was only aware of the delicious sensations that flooded his body. When Jason stiffened and put a hand on Seb's chest to push him away, cold reality struck.

"Sorry, sorry." Seb tried to climb off Jason's lap. "I didn't mean.... It's fine, we can stop...."

Jason grabbed Seb's hips and held him there. "I don't want to stop." His blue eyes were intense. "Unless you do. But the back room would be more private."

Relieved that Jason hadn't changed his mind, Seb blurted, "Oh God, yes. Of course." They weren't right by the windows, but any nosy passer-by would be able to see them if they peered in. "Let me up and we can move. Come on." He stood and took Jason's hand.

They hurried to the kitchen, Seb leading the way. Jason slammed the door shut behind them and Seb turned to face him. They were both a little breathless, and Seb wondered whether his cheeks were as flushed as Jason's. Staring at each other for a moment, they waited.

"You sure you want to do this?" Seb asked. If Jason said no, he'd kick himself for asking. But he had to be sure.

"Yeah. You?"

"Hell yes." Seb grabbed the front of Jason's sweaty T-shirt in his fist and hauled him close to kiss him again. Locked together in a passionate embrace, they stumbled backwards until Seb's arse hit the central island. As though the movement was choreographed, Jason lifted Seb so he was sitting on it and Seb wrapped his legs around Jason's waist and they kissed again.

Seb slid his hands up the back of Jason's T-shirt, finding smooth skin over firm muscle. Wanting more, he tugged the fabric upwards, breaking the kiss to get it over Jason's head. Jason started on Seb's buttons, making fast work of them, and sliding Seb's shirt off and tossing it aside while their mouths remained locked together.

Next, Jason fumbled with the button on Seb's trousers, so Seb broke the kiss to help him undo the fly. "Yours too?" he asked.

"Soon." Jason pulled the front of Seb's briefs down and wrapped his hand around Seb's cock. The rough grip of his hand robbed Seb of the ability to argue, so he moaned instead as Jason slowly slid his hand up and down. "I want to taste you."

"God yes. Please." Seb fell back on his elbows, and Jason pushed him, sliding him over the smooth stainless-steel surface so just the lower parts of his legs were hanging down. Then Jason leaned down and took Seb's dick in his mouth, sucking him deep, and making Seb's eyes roll back in his head at the sensation. "Fuck." He squeezed his eyes shut, watching Jason going down on him was almost more than he could handle, and he didn't want to come immediately.

Jason sucked Seb hard and fast, drawing off a little so he could use one hand at the base. Seb heard the sound of Jason's zip and the rustle of fabric as he freed his own erection. He opened his eyes again. The movement of Jason's arm was a tease, and Seb wished he could see more. Jason looked up and met Seb's gaze, and damn, Seb's toes curled as he fought back the urge to come.

"I'm not going to last," he warned.

Jason drew off to reply, "I don't care. I want to make you come." He licked the tip of Seb's dick before sucking him deep again and setting a fast, steady rhythm.

"That's gonna do it." Seb's muscles tightened, hips canting upwards as the wave of pleasure built and peaked. "Fuck, yes. I'm going to come," he managed to gasp.

Jason pulled off just in time, using his hand to stroke as Seb came with a groan, shooting over his stomach in thick white strands. Seb's whole body shook with the force of it.

"Good?" Jason smoothed his hand over Seb's chest. The muscles in his chest and arm flexed as he did it. He was as perfect under his T-shirt as Seb had imagined in his fantasies. Firm and strong, with a sprinkle of chest hair that Seb wanted to nuzzle.

"Amazing." Seb felt like a wrung-out dishcloth, body limp and sated. Now he'd come, he was self-conscious with Jason's gaze roving over his torso. Feeling skinny, un-toned, and inadequate compared to Jason, he wanted to distract him. At least Seb knew he was good with his mouth, and it was Jason's turn to get off. "You going to let me return the favour?"

"In a minute." Jason grabbed Seb's legs and pulled him so his arse was on the edge of the counter. As Jason straightened, his thick cock reared up, visible between Seb's thighs. He pressed it against Seb's arse and dry-humped him a few times, the movement pulling his foreskin back with each thrust as Seb watched, entranced.

"This would be the perfect height to fuck you on," Jason observed.

The idea of that made Seb's softening cock halt in its retreat and perk up again. He loved to bottom, and Jason's cock would feel incredible inside him. "God yes. If only we had lube and condoms."

"It would be a good way of testing my workmanship." Jason grinned.

"Not sure it will help me meet the hygiene requirements for the Food Standards Agency." Seb chuckled, and Jason burst out laughing.

"Yeah I guess not, but at least stainless steel is easy to clean. Bit of a wipe down and nobody would ever know."

Energised again, Seb sat up and cupped Jason's face in his hands, kissing him briefly before saying, "Come on. It's your turn now." He slipped off the counter and guided Jason around so it was his back to the unit now. Then Seb dropped to his knees on the dusty soon-to-be replaced lino floor so he was face-to-face with Jason's junk.

SIX

Jason's legs were shaky as he looked down at Seb. His trousers and pants were round his ankles, his cock was so hard it was aching, and he was desperate to come. Taking his dick in hand, he gripped it tight, and angled it towards Seb's mouth.

But Seb ducked down and pressed his nose to Jason's balls, breathing in deeply. "God, you smell good."

"Are you sure about that?" Jason asked, amused. "I reckon I must stink like a rugby player's jockstrap after half a day's training, but whatever you say." He stroked himself slowly, trying to be patient.

"I love it." Seb cupped Jason's balls with gentle fingers and nuzzled beneath them.

"Seb!" Jason tapped his dick against Seb's forehead. "Please?"

"Please what?" Seb grinned, upturned face full of mischief. He knew exactly what, but he obviously wanted to hear Jason say it.

"Please suck my cock."

"Oh well. Since you asked so nicely."

And with that, Seb parted his lips around the wet head of Jason's dick and sucked.

Jason tried to stave off his orgasm, because he wanted to make the most of the experience. But he was too turned on and the sensory overload of Seb's mouth on him, the sight of Seb on his knees, and the wet sounds of his sucking soon sent Jason spiralling beyond the point of no return.

"I'm coming." He whipped his dick away and turned slightly so that when he shot, his spunk arced away from Seb's face and splattered on the floor.

"I wanted to swallow it." Seb sounded disappointed.

"Sorry," Jason said breathlessly as he squeezed out the last drops. "But we hadn't discussed it so I thought it was better to pull out."

"Any reason I shouldn't taste your come?" Seb reached for Jason's cock and took over stroking gently.

"No. I get tested regularly and everything was fine last time."

"Good. Me too." And with that, Seb licked the come off the tip of Jason's dick before sucking him deep again a few times and then releasing him. As Seb got to his feet, Jason pulled up his underwear and jeans, but didn't bother to fasten them. Seb put his arms around Jason, lifting his face for a kiss.

"You're all sticky," Jason said. But he kissed him anyway, amused to note that Seb's cock was still sticking out of the front of his briefs and he was half-hard again. That was hot. He reached down and squeezed Seb's arse, slipping his hands under the waistband of his underwear to find warm skin. When he dipped a finger into Seb's crack and rubbed it up and down, Seb moaned, and dragged his mouth away from Jason's to mutter, "God. I wish you could fuck me."

"Another time?" Jason suggested, lips brushing Seb's neck. All his good intentions about keeping things professional had already been ruined. He may as well make the most of it now.

"You want to hook-up again?" Seb pulled back so he could meet Jason's eyes, his gaze was serious.

"Yeah. If you do." Jason shrugged, trying to be casual. But he really wanted Seb to agree to it. This encounter had only whetted his appetite, Jason definitely wanted more.

"I thought you'd be strictly a one-off kind of guy. No-strings, never speak of it again kind of thing."

"I don't mind repeats as long as you're okay with being discreet."

There was a pause, and Jason could almost see the cogs turning in Seb's head. He frowned a little as though unsure, and Jason was afraid he was going to say no.

"Yeah, okay," Seb said finally. It was clear he had some reservations.

Relief and elation rushed through Jason despite Seb's hesitance. "Great."

Seb rubbed his come into his stomach with a grimace before putting his shirt back on, and did up his fly. Jason took that as his signal to do the same, retrieving his T-shirt from the floor last before pulling it back over his head.

"Would you want to come to my place sometime?" Seb asked. His tone was as carefully casual as Jason's had been earlier, but his tense expression gave him away. Jason felt a flush of satisfaction that their attraction was obviously mutual.

"Yeah, that sounds good." Better than another risky hook-up when they were both supposed to be working, and

Jason didn't like inviting guys back to his house. He was worried his neighbours would get suspicious.

"When are you free?"

"Most evenings next week apart from Wednesday. I have my daughter then."

"How about Monday, eight o'clock?"

"Sure."

Seb smiled, looking as relieved as Jason felt to have a date lined up. Not a *date* date of course, but a day and time where they could do this again, only with lube and condoms and guaranteed privacy next time.

FEELING IN A CELEBRATORY MOOD, Seb went round to Penny and Trude's with a chilled bottle of Prosecco that evening. He had an open invitation to turn up on their doorstep any time, so although they weren't expecting him, Penny greeted him with a hug and a kiss on each cheek.

"Hello, sweetie. Happy Friday," she said. "Come in. How are you?"

"I'm fantastic thank you." Still glowing from his encounter with Jason earlier, Seb could hardly contain his high spirits. "You?"

"Glad it's Friday. Come through; Trude's out in the garden." Penny led the way into the kitchen that was on the back of the house. French windows opened onto decking at the back and the evening sun poured in. "Go on out, I'll get some glasses. Do you want it neat or do you want to join us in an Aperol Spritz? We already have a bottle open."

"Ooh, Aperol Spritz please. It seems like the weather for it."

After greeting Trude with a kiss on the cheek, Seb took a seat. "Gosh, isn't it gorgeous this evening?" He looked out at the view. Their street was high up on the hill and it dropped off steeply enough that they could see the harbour over the rooftops. Lots of boats were out enjoying the good weather, and the green slope rising on the other side of the creek was the perfect foil to the deep blue of the water and the paler blue of the sky.

"Stunning isn't it?" Trude agreed. "We're so lucky to live here."

"Yes, we are." A deep rush of contentment filled Seb. He was blessed to live in this beautiful place. For the first time he felt truly sure about his decision to leave London. No city streets could compare with this tranquil beauty.

"Here you go." Penny had returned with a tall glass filled with ice, fizzy liquid, and a chunk of orange.

"Thank you. Cheers." Seb raised his glass and took a sip. "That's lovely. It looks like Tango but it tastes wonderful."

Penny laughed. "Drink up. We're on our second already. You have some catching up to do."

"Yes ma'am." Seb grinned and took a larger gulp. "This is on an empty stomach mind you, so don't blame me if I end up talking nonsense."

"Before you get tipsy, can we talk shop for a moment?" Trude asked. "I have the draft press release ready for you to look at, unless you'd rather leave it for Monday?"

"No, I'd love to see. It doesn't feel like work because it's exciting!"

"Okay." Trude went into the kitchen and returned with an iPad. She opened it up and handed it to Seb. "Here you go."

He read it aloud with Penny and Trude listening.

"Queer-friendly café/bar coming to Porthladock.

"Rainbow Place, a new café/bar opening soon in Porthladock seeks to provide a safe and inclusive space for the LGBT community and their friends. The owner, Seb Radcliffe, recently relocated from London and feels there is a gap in the market here in Cornwall for somewhere that is openly gay-friendly. Or LGBT, which is the term Seb prefers.

"'This project is all about being inclusive, and the LGBT community is very diverse. I'd also like to be clear that the café is open to allies too. Everyone is welcome; as long as they believe LGBT people deserve equal rights and respect.'

"Rainbow Place is currently being refurbished ready for a grand opening at the end of May. It will be open from 8:30 a.m. to 11 p.m. every day, and will serve a huge range of meals, snacks, cakes, and drinks—both alcoholic and non-alcoholic. It should be an exciting addition to the already flourishing small town of Porthladock."

Seb beamed as he finished. "This is great, Trude. Really great."

"Anything you want to change?"

"I don't think so. It sums up exactly what I'm trying to do. I'm happy for it to go out like this. What do you think, Penny?"

"I think it's perfect. And I love the name Rainbow Place. I'm glad you picked that one."

"Yes. I like it too." Seb had shortlisted three names after a night of brainstorming with Penny and Trude. But Rainbow Place was the one that had stuck in his head.

"Well, if you're happy with the press release it's ready to send whenever you're ready for the news to get out," Trude said.

"Maybe the end of next week? That's around two weeks before the opening. Then we can follow up with the final press release and photos of the interior the week before the launch."

"Sounds perfect."

"If you two are done talking shop, my drink is empty." Penny held up her glass, ice cubes clinking. "And it's your turn to make them, darling."

"Your wish is my command." Trude drained her glass. "Are you ready for another one, Seb?"

"I can be. This stuff is way too easy to glug." Seb proved his point by finishing his in a few mouthfuls and handing his empty glass to Trude with a grin.

"I'd probably better get some food going to mop up all this alcohol," she said. "Do you want to eat here, Seb? We've got quiches and salads and there's plenty to go around even though Carson eats like a horse these days."

"Yes please, that would be wonderful. I must cook for you two again soon. It's been a while since the epic curry night."

While Trude was in the kitchen, Penny asked, "So, why are you so cheerful tonight?"

"Aren't I always?" Seb tried to evade the question. His first drink was already making him a little giddy and the urge to spill everything to Penny was strong. This was one of the reasons Seb had hesitated to accept Jason's offer of repeats. He was terrible at keeping secrets and hated being discreet. Generally he had a rule not to get involved with closeted men. He'd been burned that way before, getting too close to someone who could never give him what he wanted. But Jason was impossible to resist, like a terribly calorific pudding that Seb knew he'd regret eating once his plate was clean.

"Not like this. You look like a kid the night before Christmas."

"I had a good week, that's all. Work on the café is going well and I'm excited about the prospect of opening—a bit nervous too of course."

"And how is it having Jason around you all day? Have you managed to keep your hands to yourself? Or has your crush abated now you're in close proximity and the novelty's worn off."

Seb felt his cheeks heat. "The crush definitely hasn't worn off." Penny flashed a glance at him and he looked down at his hands, avoiding her penetrating gaze.

"Oh, Seb. You really like him, don't you? Is it totally unrequited?"

Cheeks positively flaming now, Seb tried to give a casual shrug. "Um, yes. Probably."

"Probably?"

"I mean definitely. I'm sure he's straight. Straighter than a straight thing," Seb babbled desperately. "I should get over it and go back to pining over celebrities instead. At least they're completely unobtainable so it's less depressing when they don't like me back. I can cope with my love for the Hemsworth brothers because I know I'm never going to have them." Seb raised his eyes again and winced when he saw the knowing expression on Penny's face.

"You're a terrible liar."

"What?" Seb made a last-ditch attempt to sound innocent.

"Something happened didn't it?"

"Fuck. Is it really that obvious?"

"You turned the colour of a beetroot as soon as I mentioned his name, you've been grinning like an idiot since you got here, and you protested way too much. So yes. It's obvious."

"What's obvious?" Trude asked, emerging from the kitchen with a tray of drinks.

"Something's going on between Seb and Jason."

"Shhhhh! I'm not supposed to tell anyone about it. God, Penny. He'd freak out if he knew I'd told you."

"You didn't tell me."

"Well, whatever. I might as well have done because you know now."

"That's fantastic though," Trude said, handing Seb a glass. "If you like him."

Grateful for the alcoholic reinforcements, he took a swig. "I *do* like him. But it's not as simple as that. He's in the closet; I'm about to open a gay café for crying out loud. There's no way this is ever going to turn into anything other than a discreet sexual arrangement, and that's not really what I'm looking for."

"Well, maybe you should steer clear then," Penny said.

"Mmm. If I was sensible, I probably would. But I'm not sensible. I'm horny and lonely, and Jason's hot, available, and unaccountably interested in me."

"Hey, don't put yourself down," Trude said. "Why wouldn't he be interested in you?"

"He could have anyone, looking like he does. He's definitely punching below his weight. I'm just being realistic." Seb's confidence had been knocked badly when his younger boyfriend had dumped him earlier that year. Since then, when Seb looked in the mirror he saw all his flaws in sharp relief where previously his brain had used soft focus.

Penny snorted. "Everyone has different tastes. If he's into you, he's into you."

"Well, maybe today was just a spur of the moment

thing. But I'm seeing him on Monday after work, so I guess I'll find out then if we really click or not."

JASON DIDN'T HAVE much time to think about his encounter with Seb until later that evening. He'd ended up leaving work a little later than planned because of their extra-curricular activities, and had raced around the supermarket before going to collect Zoe.

They spent the evening cooking together—Zoe wanted to learn how to make lasagne—and as Jason wasn't an expert it took quite a bit of concentration to pull that together. After dinner, they watched a movie. It was Zoe's choice and she picked *Freaky Friday*. They'd both seen it before as it was one of Zoe's favourites. Relieved of the need to concentrate, Jason's mind started to wander as soon as it began and immediately landed on Seb.

What the fuck was I thinking?

Jason kicked himself for shitting on his own doorstep. Giving in to his attraction to Seb was an impulse he should have curbed, because it threatened his neatly compartmentalised life. Normally he only ever had sex with guys who lived a little way away. He wasn't into passing his hook-ups in the street and pretending they were strangers. It was awkward and weird and made him anxious about discovery.

He was also worried about Seb's motives. His hesitance when Jason had insisted on discretion implied it wasn't something he was used to. And why would it be? Seb was out and didn't hide his sexuality. He was probably looking for a boyfriend, not a secret fuck buddy. Guilt nagged at Jason along with his anxiety. Seb deserved better than this, but he was a grown man and this was his choice as much as Jason's.

Yet somehow, despite his misgivings, Jason couldn't regret what had happened with Seb that afternoon. As he remembered it now—in great and glorious detail—he had to work hard to stop a smile spreading over his face and giving him away. He stared resolutely at the screen, forcing his expression to remain impassive while his brain replayed every kiss, every touch, the expression on Seb's face as he came, the sight of him with his lips wrapped around Jason's cock.

And we get to do it again on Monday.

Just three days to wait. Jason wanted to roll his eyes at himself for counting. He couldn't remember the last time he'd looked forward to a repeat with such anticipation. Normally he was happy to see the same guy more than once, but mainly only because it was convenient. He'd never felt much connection with anyone, even with guys he'd met several times. It already felt different with Seb.

WHEN MONDAY MORNING finally came around, Jason's stomach was fluttering with nerves as he let himself and Will into the café. They usually arrived before Seb, and sure enough the place was still dark and deserted.

"Let's get started then," Jason said eager to get stuck into work to occupy his brain. He'd spent far more time this weekend thinking about Seb than he was comfortable with. Freaked out by the level of his interest, he'd considered cancelling their plans for today. But now the day had come he couldn't bring himself to do it.

"What's up first today, boss?" Will asked.

"We need to lay the new lino in the kitchen. When

that's done we can get started on the main room if we have any time left."

Occupied with fitting the new flooring, Jason managed to push thoughts of Seb aside for a while. With the radio playing pop music he didn't hear Seb arrive, and it wasn't until a voice said cheerily, "Good morning, chaps. How are you today?" that he realised Seb was there.

Immediately, Jason's heart raced, and his ears glowed as if they were sunburned. "Alright, Seb. Not bad thanks, mate. You?" His voice came out gruff and excessively macho to his own ears, and given Seb's raised eyebrows he noticed it too. Thankfully Will seemed completely unaware of Jason's awkwardness, because he was too busy being awkward himself as he grunted and gave Seb a brief nod before getting back to what he was doing.

"I'm fine thank you." Seb's smile was a little cautious. "Everything okay? I'm interviewing potential chefs and chef assistants, so I'll use the main room as long as you're working in here."

Jason sat back on his heels. "We'll be in here this morning, but might need to work the main room later. Is that a problem? Only once we're done with the lino it needs to be left for twenty-four hours, so we'll have to stay out of the kitchen. We were going to make a start on cleaning and filling the walls ready for painting, but at least that won't be too noisy."

"No problem. If you start at the far end, I can carry on interviewing and you won't disturb us." Seb paused, as though he had more to say. Standing, he was looking down at Jason and his gaze slid over Jason's torso and back to his face. Jason's heart skipped a beat as he remembered their positions reversed on Friday, with Seb kneeling at his feet.

Locked in a silence that was loaded, Seb was the one to finally break it. "My first chef applicant is due soon. Is it okay with you if I bring them in to show them the kitchen?"

"Of course. Not that there's much to see yet."

"I'm sure any chef will see the potential. Okay, thanks. I'll leave you to it for now. See you later."

With that, Seb hurried away. Jason couldn't help noticing that his arse was looking particularly fine today in a pair of snug teal chinos. He hoped Seb would wear them this evening too.

SEVEN

Seb wasn't as focused on the interviews as he should have been. While his candidates were talking about their menu ideas, and telling him about their relevant experience, Seb's mind was wandering into the back room and imagining Jason on his hands and knees laying lino. Seb wished *he* was getting laid by Jason; hopefully tonight that fantasy would become reality.

Desperate for a chance to confirm their plans, Seb was hoping to catch Jason alone. But so far he'd been thwarted in his attempts. Every time he'd popped into the kitchen between interviews, Will had been there too. Lunchtime was approaching, though, when Will usually went out for a fag break. Hopefully Seb could talk to Jason then.

Sure enough, shortly after midday Will passed through the front room. Jason was just wrapping up his interview with a charming Italian called Luca. He was applying for the job of chef and was one of Seb's favourites so far.

"Okay, Luca. It was a pleasure to meet you, and I really like your ideas for the menu. I'll be in touch as soon as I've made a decision. Do you have any questions for me?" Seb mentally crossed his fingers hoping Luca wouldn't.

"No, Mr Radcliffe. I don't think so," Luca said. His accent was gorgeous. In fact Luca was gorgeous, with his dark curls and stubble, and intense brown eyes. Normally Seb would have been all a-flutter being faced with such a delicious specimen of manhood, but today he only had eyes for Jason. He didn't get a gay vibe from Luca anyway, so he suspected that any interest would definitely have been one-sided.

"Right." Seb stood and offered Luca his hand, signalling that the interview was over.

Luca shook and Seb saw him out, watching his retreating form as he walked down the street. He was definitely the best contender so far for the chef's job; the final candidate this afternoon would have to be seriously impressive to beat Luca. Seb hoped Luca would accept the job if it was offered to him.

After some deliberation and discussion with Trude, Seb had decided not to disclose at interview that the café was to be an LGBT-focused one. They didn't want anyone to spread the word before they were ready. But Seb was going to inform the people he actually offered jobs to. He felt it was best that all the staff he employed were totally on board with his plans, and would prefer not to have anyone working there who wasn't one hundred per cent supportive. He'd deliberately dressed for the interviews in a way that he hoped signalled queer-as-fuck, teaming a pink short-sleeved button-down with his skinny-fit chinos, assuming that he'd pick up on any negative vibes from candidates who weren't comfortable with him. The rainbow pin on his pocket was maybe overkill, but it was best to be sure.

As Seb stepped back into the dim interior of the café, he

felt a thrill of nerves and excitement. He and Jason were finally alone. As though it was planned, Jason emerged from the kitchen with a box of tools in one hand as Seb approached.

"Oh, hi." He stopped in the doorway when he saw Seb.

"How's it going?" Seb asked his voice unnaturally bright. Nerves had tightened his throat.

"Good. The lino's all down now. It needs to be left to set till tomorrow so we should stay out of the kitchen for the rest of the day."

"Can I see?"

"Of course." Jason stood aside so Seb could come and take a look.

"It looks brilliant!" Seb said, excited. The black and white chessboard pattern he'd chosen looked great with the shiny silver of the stainless-steel counters.

"Yeah. I like the black and white." Jason's voice came from just behind Seb, and Seb's skin prickled with the awareness of his proximity.

Turning, Seb plucked up the courage to ask the question he'd wanted to ask all day. "So... are we still on for tonight?"

Jason's slight hesitation made disappointment swoop in Seb's stomach.

Fuck, he's changed his mind.

He braced himself to be let down gently, already preparing the breezy phrases he'd use to hide how disappointed he was.

"Yeah. I think so. If you are?" Jason's uncertainty wasn't totally reassuring, but it was better than an outright no.

"I've been looking forward to it," Seb said honestly. He didn't see the point in playing it cool. One of them needed to be decisive here.

That seemed to be the right response, because Jason's face relaxed into a smile. "Yes. So have I."

"Eight o'clock at mine then?"

Jason nodded. "I don't know your address."

"I'll text it to you."

They ran out of things to say, and that now-familiar tension was back as they stared at each other. Jason licked his lips nervously and Seb longed to kiss him. But the front door stood open, and they couldn't go into the kitchen. He'd have to wait till tonight.

Jason finally broke the silence. "I'm heading out to buy some lunch. Do you want me to get you anything?"

"Where are you going? I can't have another pasty, not in these trousers. They're already snug."

Jason's lips quirked as he let his gaze rove down over Seb. "They look damn good on you. I can get you something from the deli instead if you want?"

"Okay, thanks. I'll have a chicken salad sandwich on wholegrain. No mayo. And can you get me a skinny vanilla latte too please?"

"Of course." Jason put down the toolbox and headed out into the sunlight.

As Seb watched Jason leave, disappointment tempered his excitement about tonight. He'd have liked to have gone with him. After being indoors all morning he could do with some fresh air, but he didn't want to make Jason uncomfortable. He probably wouldn't want to be seen with Seb in his pink shirt and rainbow pin.

THE AFTERNOON WENT BY QUICKLY, much to Seb's relief.

As he suspected, the other head chef candidate didn't

measure up to Luca, so he phoned Luca to offer him the job. When he explained about the theme of the café Luca was totally unfazed.

"Whatever. It's all fine with me. I don't care if people are gay, bi, straight. As long as they are nice people. And if they are working in my kitchen all I care is that they do a good job."

"In that case, you're hired." Seb grinned at Luca's words. "I'll email you the contract tomorrow."

After that, Seb offered the assistant chef job to a woman called Amelia. She was young, but she'd impressed Seb with her enthusiasm and friendly nature. Her references had been very good, and she had plenty of experience in hotels and cafés so should be able to cope with the pressure. She was also very keen on baking and was happy to take on the responsibility for the cake menu. He hoped she and Luca would make an excellent team.

Even better, when he offered her the job and told her about the details of the café she interrupted excitedly, "Oh, that's amazing. What a brilliant idea."

"I'm glad you think so," Seb said, delighted.

"I'm actually bisexual. I'm currently in a monogamous relationship with a guy, so a lot of people don't know that about me. But I'm open about it if it comes up. Seriously though, I'm super excited you've offered me the job—even more so now I know about this. I grew up in St Austell and there was nothing for queer kids of my generation. We need things like this."

WHEN SEB GOT HOME, he was in high spirits. Happy with the two staff members he'd hired today, he was feeling more positive about his plans for Rainbow Place than ever.

With the prospect of some hopefully amazing sex with Jason tonight, he couldn't have been in a better mood if he'd won the lottery.

After making himself a quick snack, Seb changed his bed, showered, and got himself squeaky clean in all the places he hoped would be utilised later that evening. They hadn't explicitly discussed what they were into, but after Jason's comment about the worktop being the perfect height for fucking Seb on, Seb was pretty sure Jason would be up for topping him. His arse clenched in delighted anticipation at the thought of Jason's cock.

Seb put his teal chinos back on. They weren't ones Seb wore often, he felt a little self-conscious about wearing skinny-fit trousers at his age. He didn't want to be ram dressed as lamb, but Jason had admired them so he obviously didn't think Seb was too old to look good in them. He teamed them with a pale grey polo shirt in a soft fabric and left his feet bare. Then he went down to make sure his living room was tidy.

It was immaculate. Seb was a neat freak by his own admission. Robbed of the opportunity for distraction, Seb put a chilled-out music playlist on and paced anxiously until the doorbell finally rang, five minutes after eight.

Heart fluttering like a bird trapped in a cage, Seb hurried to the door and opened it with a hand that was sticky with nerves. He was never normally this nervous about meeting up with guys.

Jason stood on the doorstep looking equally tense. "Hi." He glanced up and down the street as though afraid someone might see him. Of course, he probably was. It was unfortunate for Jason that it was still light outside at this time of year; being seen going into Seb's house wouldn't exactly help him stay in the closet.

"Come in." Seb ushered him inside, pushing aside his resentment at feeling like a guilty secret. It wasn't his place to tell any other queer person when and how to come out. It was Jason's choice to be discreet and Seb had to respect that if he wanted to be involved with him.

Jason sweetened the pill by surprising Seb with a kiss as soon as they were inside. He cupped Seb's cheeks in his large hands and kissed him so thoroughly that Seb forgot everything except the soft brush of Jason's lips and the warmth of his palms.

"I've wanted to do that all day," Jason said as he drew away, a goofy smile on his face that made Seb's heart flip.

"Me too." He grinned back. "So, um... would you like a drink of anything? Tea, coffee, beer, wine?" Nervous, Seb could use a glass of wine, but he didn't want to dull his senses too much.

"No thanks." Jason looked Seb over in a way that felt like a caress. "I'm glad you're still wearing those trousers. They make your arse look gorgeous."

Seb flushed with pleasure at the compliment. "Thank you. You look good too." Jason was in dark jeans, slimmer-fit ones than he wore for work, and they emphasised the length of his legs and the muscles in his thighs. An olive green T-shirt hugged his torso to perfection. The heat in his eyes matched the building anticipation that buzzed through Seb's veins like electricity. "Do you want to sit in the living room for a while?" He paused for a beat before blurting, "Or we could go straight upstairs if you prefer."

"Straight upstairs sounds good to me. Although there's nothing straight about what we're going to be doing when we get there." Jason grinned.

The last bit of Seb's tension dropped away as he

laughed. "I'm glad to hear it." He took Jason's hand and tugged him towards the stairs. "Come on then."

Jason followed Seb up the narrow staircase. "It almost seems a shame that I'm going to be taking those trousers off you soon. Mind you, I bet your bum looks good naked too."

"Well I haven't had any complaints so far." Seb opened the door to his bedroom and turned to pull Jason into a kiss.

Their lips met, opening hungrily to taste each other. Somehow Seb's hands found their way under the front of Jason's T-shirt to stroke his chest while Jason went straight for Seb's arse, cupping and squeezing through his clothes. Soon Seb was hard and he could feel the rigid bulge of Jason's dick grinding against his stomach, so he knew he wasn't the only one.

Wanting more skin to explore, Seb pushed Jason's T-shirt up, breaking the kiss to pull it over Jason's head as he lifted his arms to help. Then he stripped off his own before kissing Jason again. With warm skin against warm skin, and the scratch of Jason's chest hair under his fingertips, Seb was in heaven.

Jason tried to get a hand down the back of Seb's trousers but they were too tight, so Seb undid the button and zip to help him. The sensation of Jason's work-roughened palm sliding over the sensitive skin of his butt cheek made Seb moan and press back into it. He was rewarded by Jason's finger pushing into his crack. Jason's mouth was on Seb's neck now, and he muttered between kisses, "Please tell me you bottom?"

"Oh fuck, yes," Seb said.

"Good. I was pretty sure I was reading the signals right." Jason rubbed his finger over Seb's hole, making him squirm and gasp. "You want my dick in there?"

"Well I don't know what gave you the idea that I'm a

greedy, cock-hungry bottom," Seb managed breathlessly. "But you're right."

Jason's low chuckle was like warm honey as he drew back and spun a finger at Seb. "Turn around then."

So turned on that his legs felt weak, Seb obeyed, turning his back to Jason and waiting to see what Jason would do next. Gripping Seb's hips with firm hands, Jason got to his knees and pulled Seb's trousers down. "Sexy briefs." Skimpy and purple with a white elastic waistband, they were one of Seb's favourite pairs so he was glad Jason appreciated them. "But they have to go too."

Painfully slowly, Jason eased them down over Seb's arse. He kissed the skin as it was exposed, switching from cheek to cheek until he'd got them down around Seb's knees along with his trousers. Seb was so hard that his foreskin had drawn right back to show the pink head of his cock, already wet at the tip. Jason's kisses gradually zeroed in closer and closer to where Seb wanted his mouth. He fought the urge to spread his cheeks, enjoying giving Jason the control. It was fascinating seeing him being so forceful when he was usually on the quiet side. Sex always showed another side of a man, and Seb loved how you could never predict what someone would be like in the sack until you actually got naked with them.

Jason pushed him towards the bed and Seb put out his arms, bracing himself on the edge of it. "Yeah, that's perfect. Now spread your legs a bit.... There." Jason grabbed Seb's arse and opened him up, licking into Seb's crack with a hum of pleasure. "This okay?"

"Hell yes."

Jason licked deeper, his tongue finding Seb's hole and focusing on it with slow, wet circles.

Spreading his legs wider, Seb pushed back against the

warmth of Jason's tongue. Jason groaned as though he was the one having his arse licked and reached between Seb's legs to stroke his cock. Seb made a sound that was embarrassingly like a whimper, but it was all he could manage. His senses were overwhelmed by the grip of Jason's hand, and the increasingly urgent thrusts of his tongue. It was wonderful, but sweet torture because he wanted more; harder, deeper, rougher. His body was craving to be filled. He moaned, wordless desperation as he tried to be patient.

As though Jason could read his mind, he got a finger to Seb's spit-wet hole, and pushed it inside. It went in easily and Seb welcomed it. "Fuck, yes. More."

Jason slid his finger in and out a few times before withdrawing it and making Seb groan with frustration.

"You really are a greedy bottom." Jason's voice was rough and a little breathless. "Do you need lube yet?"

"No. Just use more spit." Seb didn't want to move and break the spell. He could take two fingers without lube. Sometimes he enjoyed the extra friction; the edge of pain was a thrill that only added to his pleasure. Looking back over his shoulder, he watched as Jason sucked on two fingers before working them into Seb.

"God you feel tight. Are you sure that doesn't hurt?"

"Nah. It's good." Seb squeezed his muscles and then released them, his body accepting the intrusion as Jason pushed deeper. "Oh fuck." Jason's fingers felt incredible and his hand on Seb's dick, stroking slowly, soon had Seb thrusting into his grip and then back onto his fingers as he lost himself completely in the sensations that were taking over his body. Sweat prickled on his back and his balls tingled, heavy with the need to come, but he fought it back, biting his lip to distract himself.

"You look so hot," Jason said. "I can't wait to see you take my cock."

"Do it. I want it."

"Yeah? Where do you want it?"

"In my arse." Seb was desperate now. "Please. Fuck me."

"Where's your lube and condoms?"

"In the drawer by the bed."

The loss of Jason's fingers and hand made Seb feel as though he was emerging from underwater. Suddenly he was aware of his surroundings rather than being totally focused on his body. The evening sun slanted in through his window, bright on the duck-egg blue of his duvet cover. Naked, Seb felt exposed as Jason walked over to the drawer, still in his jeans. But Seb resisted the urge to move and cover himself. Instead he waited where Jason had left him, bent at the waist, his hands braced on the bed.

After tossing the lube and a condom down on the bed, Jason turned to face Seb. "You want this?" He palmed the obvious bulge in his jeans.

"Yes." Seb wanted it so badly it was like starvation.

Painfully slowly, Jason unbuttoned his fly and then slid the zip down to reveal the jutting ridge of his dick in pale grey boxers with a wet patch at the head. He rubbed it through the fabric.

"Show me," Seb begged.

"I'll do more than show you." Jason pushed down his jeans and boxers, letting his thick cock spring free. He gripped it in his fist, stroking slowly. "Get on the bed, on your hands and knees."

Seb scrambled to comply, his arse aching to be filled.

Jason climbed on the bed in front of him, finally naked.

He knelt in front of Seb. "Suck it. Show me how much you want it."

Seb opened his mouth eagerly, moaning as he let Jason push inside. He tasted of precome and when he thrust deep, saliva pooled in Seb's mouth. He sucked, forcing himself to keep Jason in his throat until the need for oxygen had him pulling off and gasping. He went more cautiously next time, focusing on the head and swirling his tongue around, feeling every ridge and vein.

"That's so good," Jason said, putting his hand on the back of Seb's head and pushing him down so Seb had to take him deep again. "So fucking good. But I want to stick it in your arse. Do you want that too?"

"Mmmmm," Seb hummed something he hoped sounded like emphatic agreement around his mouthful of dick. "Mmph."

Chuckling, Jason pulled away. "Okay then." He picked up the condom and lube and moved behind Seb. "Finger yourself while I get this on."

Reaching around, Seb pushed two fingers into his hole. He groaned in frustration, unable to get them deep enough. "Want your cock."

"I know you do. It's coming."

Seb snorted. "Hopefully not yet."

Jason's laughter warmed him from the inside. "No, not yet. Although it might not take long. You look so sexy on your hands and knees for me, it's going to be hard to make it last. If I come too quickly, I'll blow you after." He pressed the head of his cock against Seb's hole, sliding it up and down in a delicious tease. "You ready?"

"*Yes.*"

With that, Jason filled him in one firm thrust that stole

Seb's breath. Tensing, Seb gripped the duvet cover, creasing it in his fists.

Jason held still, balls-deep, his breathing ragged. "Okay?"

"Yeah," Seb gasped. "It's good, just... intense." The stretch felt impossible, as though it was too much for his body to handle. But Seb knew from experience that it would soon give way to something easier, something that would be incredible. The grip of Jason's hands on his hips grounded him, and as Jason gently slid out and then back, it was like a key slotting into place and unlocking new heights of pleasure. "Oh fuck, yes. That's so good."

Jason went a little faster, then a little harder, reading Seb's wordless sounds of pleasure and responding to them. He put one hand on Seb's shoulder, holding him in place as he slammed into him in a relentless, perfect rhythm.

Seb held off from touching his cock, wanting to focus on the feeling of Jason fucking him for as long as he could before he gave in to the urge to come. But soon he couldn't wait any longer. Dropping down onto one elbow so he could reach down to jerk himself off, he gasped, "I'm really close now."

He closed his hand around his cock, stroking himself hard and fast as Jason pistoned into him, grunting with each thrust. It only took a few strokes before white-hot pleasure detonated and Seb came, groaning and shooting all over the bed beneath him as Jason fucked him through it. Then Jason made a strangled sound and stilled, his cock pulsing where it was buried deep inside Seb, fingers biting into Seb's hip and shoulder. "Oh fuck, yes," he groaned. "Jesus, Seb." He released his grip, gently sliding his hands over Seb's skin. "God, I hope I didn't leave bruises."

"I don't care if you did," Seb managed weakly. "Totally worth it."

Jason slid free from Seb and moved to get a box of tissues from by the bed. He passed them to Seb to mop up his mess. Seb turned the now-sticky duvet back and flopped down on the sheet, hoping Jason would join him. This might only be a hook-up, but Seb liked cuddles after sex.

He wasn't disappointed. As soon as Jason had binned the condom, he came and lay beside Seb, letting Seb slide into his arms like he belonged there.

EIGHT

Jason liked the weight of Seb's head on his shoulder, and the scent of his hair. He tightened his arm around Seb and pressed a kiss to the top of his head.

"That was good sex," Seb said dreamily. "Really top quality."

"Good to know. I aim to please." Jason smiled, although Seb wouldn't see it. "And it was bloody fantastic for me too."

Seb lifted his head, and his grin matched Jason's. "Yay." He climbed on top of Jason, bracketing him with his knees and arms, and lowered his face so he could kiss Jason on the lips before asking, "Does that mean you want to do it again?" His expression was open and honest.

Jason's heart beat faster, a thrill of excitement and happiness rising inside him like the tide. It was a good feeling, but scary too. Seb was making him break all his rules: too local, too openly gay, too much of a connection—in more ways than one. They worked together, but it was the intimacy already forming that Jason feared the most. He didn't want to care too deeply because that would threaten the status quo. He tried to think of a way to let Seb down gently, but the idea of not getting to do this again, not getting to fuck Seb, not getting to lie in bed with him and hold him close afterwards.... Jason couldn't bring himself to end things already.

"Yes. As long as you're still okay with it being casual and discreet."

The shutters came down, muting Seb's bright smile with a shadow of disappointment. "Of course."

He climbed off Jason to lie beside him again. Their arms were still touching, but Jason missed the full-body contact of before. He felt like a bastard for reminding Seb of the limits of their arrangement, but he'd been honest with Seb from the start. This was all Jason could offer him, for now at least.

"I'm sorry," Jason said quietly, taking Seb's hand.

"No need to be sorry." The false brightness in Seb's voice didn't make Jason feel any better. "We can have some fun together. It's fine."

The mood between them had soured, and Jason knew it was his fault but it wasn't something he could easily fix. "I guess I should head home, early start again tomorrow."

"Okay." Seb squeezed his hand briefly before releasing it.

They rolled away from each other and started dressing.

"Do you want to meet up again soon?" Jason felt as though he needed to be the one to push for more. He sensed a lack of confidence in Seb and that made him want to reassure him as much as he could, even if he couldn't give him what he really wanted.

"Yeah, I'd like that," Seb replied.

"When?"

"How about Thursday? You have your daughter with

you on Wednesday, right?"

"Yes." Jason was impressed Seb had remembered. "Thursday's good for me." It seemed a long way off, but maybe that was for the best. Hopefully they could keep things professional between now and then.

Both dressed now, there was an awkward pause as they faced each other. Seb's bed was a barricade between them, the turned-down duvet and dents in the pillows the only evidence of their former intimacy.

"Okay then. I'll be off. Thanks; that was fun." Jason winced at his clumsy words, but saying goodbye after a hook-up was always awkward.

"I'll see you out."

They made their way downstairs, the mood between them very different to the playful teasing on their way up. Jason paused before opening the front door, and Seb seemed surprised when Jason kissed him. He responded though and a little of the distance between them melted away as he relaxed into Jason's embrace.

"I had a great time," Seb said before pressing a final chaste kiss to Jason's lips. "See you in the morning."

JASON'S PHONE rang as he was walking home. It was Anna.

"Hi, is everything okay?" he asked. She didn't tend to call for casual conversation.

"Yes. Where are you?"

"Out. But I'm on my way home, why?"

"I'm on your doorstep. Will you be long?"

"Ten minutes or so." Porthladock was a small town so although Seb lived on the opposite side it wasn't a long walk. "Why are you on my doorstep?"

"Sorry. I should have called to check you were in, but you don't usually go out much in the evening. Zoe needs a book for her homework and she left it at yours so I came to pick it up for her."

"Okay, well like I said. I'll be back soon. Are you okay to wait? If not I can drop it round to yours later."

"I'll wait."

"See you in a few then."

When Jason reached his house, Anna's car was bumped up on the kerb outside and she was leaning against the car with her phone in her hand.

"Hey," Jason greeted her.

"Oh, hi." Anna smiled, putting her phone away, and stepping forward to give him a kiss on the cheek. "Sorry to turn up without calling first. I shouldn't have assumed you'd be in."

"No worries. Like you say, I usually am." Jason unlocked his door. "Come in."

"You look more spruced up than usual. Hot date?"

Jason froze, the immediate instinct to deny it warring with the urge to talk about Seb. He knew he could get away with ignoring Anna; she wouldn't pry if he didn't respond. But keeping secrets was lonely. Cautiously, he said, "Yeah. Sort of."

"Really?" Anna's surprise showed she hadn't expected him to bite. "I hope it went well."

Jason turned to meet Anna's encouraging smile. "I think it did."

"Are you seeing him again?"

A snort of laughter escaped. "It would be hard not to, given that it was the guy I told you about. Seb, remember? The bloke whose café I'm working on. But yeah, we're seeing each other out of work again soon." Heart beating fast at the admission, Jason couldn't hold back his grin.

"Wow. That's different for you. Spending time with someone local. I assume nobody else knows."

"No, and I want it to stay that way."

"Of course. How do you feel about it?"

"Mixed feelings I guess." Jason shrugged. "I like him. But getting involved with someone so close to home makes me nervous."

"I can understand that." Jason was grateful that Anna didn't launch into another attempt at encouraging him to be open about his sexuality. He knew she meant well, but her support sometimes felt like pressure. "But as long as you trust him, then you can just wait and see how it goes. You don't need to rush into any decisions."

"I suppose." The idea of a future past their next date wasn't something Jason had considered until now. He'd been focused on the present, not looking ahead to how this relationship with Seb might develop—or how it might end. Typical of Anna to jump straight to the future. She'd always been a planner, liking to explore what might happen next rather than live in the moment. Jason felt more comfortable dealing with the reality of now.

"Well, I'd better go up and find that book. I left Zoe washing up but she wants to get started on this homework before bed."

"Okay."

Jason went to the fridge and got himself a beer while Anna went up to Zoe's room. She came back down a few minutes later and Jason met her at the bottom of the stairs.

"Found it." She held up the book. "She needs it for an essay on World War One. I'll leave you in peace. Have a nice evening—what's left of it."

"Thanks, you too."

They hugged goodbye, and Anna let herself out.

Jason took his beer through to the living room and turned on the TV. His head was full of Seb, but thinking about Seb made Jason feel a disturbing blend of excited, anxious, and unsettled. He needed a break from it. TV would provide a distraction, and alcohol would dull the sharp edges of his emotions.

ON THE MORNING after their hook-up, Jason felt uncomfortable around Seb. With Will there like Jason's shadow while they worked on filling cracks and holes in the plaster, there was no chance to speak to Seb privately during the first part of the morning. Aware of Seb watching him sometimes, but afraid of giving himself away, Jason found himself avoiding Seb's gaze, and that made him feel even more awkward. It was weird acting like strangers after the intimacy of the night before.

When they ran out of Polyfilla, Jason was relieved instead of annoyed because it gave him the excuse to send Will out to get more. He gave Will the van keys. "Here you go. Get a couple of tubes; we're going to need it. And can you get more sandpaper too?"

"Sure."

"See you in a bit then."

As Will passed him, Seb glanced up from the table where he was working on his laptop. Then as soon as Will had gone, he came over to where Jason was smearing filler into a section of the wall.

"Hi," he said, giving Jason an uncertain smile.

Jason put his tools down and turned to face him. "Hi."

They stared at each other awkwardly for a minute.

"Are you still okay? With what happened last night, and everything?" Seb asked.

"Yeah. Last night was great." Just thinking about it made Jason's dick tingle and thicken.

Seb looked relieved. "Yes, it was. Glad you still think so."

"It's weird trying to act normal around you though," Jason admitted.

"Oh God yes. I'm struggling too. I keep wanting to touch you, and then remembering that I can't." Seb's gaze flickered down to Jason's crotch and he licked his lips.

Arousal hit Jason like a punch in the gut. Before he had time to think better of it, he said, "You could touch me now."

A slow grin spread over Seb's face and his eyes filled with mischief. "How long have we got?"

"Half an hour, tops."

"Easy. I bet I can make you come in less than five minutes."

"Sounds like a challenge."

"Come on then." Seb hurried to the back of the café.

"Not in the kitchen!" Jason said. "The glue there needs a few more hours to set. The toilet's okay though." They'd be less likely to be caught in there too; at least there was a lock on the door.

Seb opened the door to the small toilet next to the kitchen. No work had been done in there yet. The plumber was coming to replace the old chipped porcelain toilet and sink later that week, and they'd lay the new flooring after that. The rather grotty setting didn't seem to deter Seb. He shut the toilet lid and sat on it, facing Jason. "Get over here, and get your cock out." Jason squeezed around the door and locked it behind them before following Seb's instructions, while Seb unfastened his own trousers and got his dick out, stiffening in his hand as he stroked himself. "Put it in my mouth. And I want to swallow this time, so don't pull out."

Jason obeyed, his cock hard with anticipation before it even touched Seb's lips. He groaned as Seb sucked him, clearly determined to make this quick.

It probably didn't even take close to five minutes. Seb worked Jason expertly, sucking him deep and fast. He jerked himself off with one hand while he went to town on Jason's cock, and Jason's focus was torn between the sight of Seb's flushed cheeks and wet lips, and the motion of his hand on his dick. Jason's climax built fast and intense, and he gripped Seb's hair when he came, filling his mouth while Seb kept on sucking until Jason was done.

"God that was hot. I'm close now too," Seb gasped, hand flying over his cock.

Jason dropped to his knees and took Seb in his mouth. Seb moaned, and Jason only managed a few slides of his mouth before Seb came too, bitter-salt exploding on Jason's tongue as Seb's hips jerked up and his whole body tensed. "Fuck!"

After swallowing, Jason grinned up at him, and Seb leaned down for a quick kiss. "That was fun." His face was flushed and full of mischief. "I like sneaking around."

The reality of the situation hit Jason now the urge to come had passed. He stood up quickly and started fastening his trousers. "It's risky though. I don't want Will to catch us leaving the toilet together."

"Would he really be that shocked?" Seb stayed sitting, rearranging his clothes where he was.

"I have no idea how he'd react. But I don't want to find out. When I come out I want it to be on my terms, not be the subject of local gossip for being caught in the act."

"*When* you come out?" Seb stood to face Jason, eyebrows raised.

Jason realised this was the first time he'd ever thought in terms of *when* rather than *if*. He shrugged. "I guess it's bound to happen eventually. But I'm not in a rush."

"Fair enough. Well I'm sure we can manage to behave ourselves here in future," Seb said briskly. "This was your idea just now, remember?"

"I know." Jason felt guilty, as though he'd used Seb in some way, even though Seb had been totally on board with fooling around.

Brushing some non-existent dust off his trousers, Seb avoided Jason's eyes. "We should get out of here. You go first, check the coast is clear."

Reaching out to cup Seb's cheek, Jason gently guided his chin up till their gazes locked again. "I'm sorry. You deserve better. I'd understand if you didn't want to bother with me."

"It's just a bit of fun." Seb shrugged. "Stop worrying, and stop apologising. It's getting tedious. I'm a big boy and I don't need you to put a ring on it. Anytime I get bored of the secrecy I can call it quits and move on." His tone was brittle.

Jason's guts lurched at the thought of Seb ending things. He knew it was ridiculous; he had no right to expect any loyalty from him. "Okay. So we're still on for Thursday then?"

"Of course. Let's assume it's on unless one of us says otherwise." Seb's smile was back, too bright to be completely convincing.

The connection between them felt as fragile as a piece of glass. Jason was afraid that one wrong move could make the whole thing shatter.

NINE

By Thursday Seb was tired and stressed.

The week had been an emotional rollercoaster. Monday night had been a high point, the sexual chemistry between him and Jason was spectacular and in the immediate aftermath Seb had felt a connection that he craved more of. But Jason's reminder of the need for secrecy was like a pin in the balloon of Seb's post-coital happiness, leaving him deflated and flat.

Furious with himself for not being able to separate his emotions from the spectacular sex, Seb was determined to keep things purely physical. The quick-and-dirty blowjob in the toilet had seemed like a perfect way of establishing that this was all about fun, and not about feelings. Yet again, Jason had spoiled things in the aftermath by worrying about being caught—when it had been his bloody idea in the first place.

Since Tuesday they'd barely spoken, keeping their focus entirely on work-related topics. They'd both behaved perfectly, keeping their hands to themselves, and Seb had even resisted the constant urge to flirt. The sexual tension was constant, building like a wave gathering strength. Seb could see it in the heat of Jason's gaze when he caught him watching Seb occasionally, and he could feel it in his growing impatience as the hours crawled by.

The only distraction was Seb's growing anxiety about the response to the initial press release for the café. In an act of perfect—or terrible—timing, Trude had decided that Thursday was the perfect day to send it out. She was hoping the local papers, websites, and radio stations would use the story on Friday. Seb was in a whirlwind of conflicting emotions about that in perfect counterpoint to his mixed feelings about Jason. Excited about the step forward and hoping the press release would kick-start lots of publicity and visibility for the café, he was also shitting himself about what the overall tone of the reaction would be. Prepared for some negativity, he was hoping it would be balanced by genuine interest and support, but there was no way of telling until it happened.

Late on Thursday afternoon, he and Trude were sitting at his makeshift desk near the front window of the café, laptop in front of them. Jason and Will were busy painting a wall on the other side of the room. The smell of matt emulsion was strong, but with the windows and doors open the through-draft stopped it from being overpowering.

"Are you ready to send it?" Trude asked.

"I think so." Seb felt sick and his hand trembled where it was poised over the enter key. They'd read and re-read the press release what felt like a thousand times, tweaking and editing until it became a collection of sentences that lost all meaning in the way that a single word looks unrecognisable if you stare at it for too long.

"It's as good as it can possibly be," Trude said with a confidence that Seb envied. "Do it."

"You sure?"

She nodded, dark eyes amused at Seb's hesitance.

Pulse thundering in his ears, Seb hit send. "I think I'm going to puke," he muttered as his laptop made the *whoosh* sound of an email being sent. "Now what do I do?"

"Sit back and wait. Some of them might contact you if they want more details, but most of them will probably just run the story as you gave it to them. With a bit of luck there'll be something in the paper tomorrow, or over the weekend. It's a good story for local news organisations; I think they'll want to use it soon. Let's hope the response is mostly positive."

"Yes." Seb's stomach lurched again. "Well. It's done. And now the secret's out I can start advertising for more staff. I'll do that before I go home today too."

"Yes, only a couple of weeks before the launch now. Lots to organise." Trude smiled, her excitement helping to ignite Seb's enthusiasm again. She was helping Seb plan the grand opening; they'd be publicising that nearer the time too. Checking her watch, she said, "Right. I need to head off. I have a meeting with Carson's tutor after school today, so I'd better hurry."

Seb stood to see her out. "Thanks, Trude. See you soon."

"Dinner on Saturday if not before."

"Of course." Seb made a mental note to go shopping for ingredients tomorrow. He hadn't forgotten he'd invited them, but had been so preoccupied he hadn't thought about what to cook yet.

Sitting back at his laptop, Seb drafted job ads for serving staff and kitchen assistants and posted them on local job websites. Then he texted a lady called Bev who had been recommended as a reliable cleaner.

With most of his to-do list done for the day, Seb's attention wandered, and inevitably settled on Jason. With his back to Seb, he was using a roller to cover a large section of wall in the pale terracotta paint Seb had chosen for the main interior walls. The vigorous movement showed off the play of muscle in Jason's back through the thin T-shirt he was wearing. The fabric clung where he was sweating and Seb drifted off into fantasy, imagining peeling it off and feeling the shape of those muscles with his hands.

Tonight, he thought. *Tonight I get to touch him again.*

Perhaps he could get Jason to fuck him face-to-face this time. Seb liked the idea of being on his back, legs wrapped around Jason's hips. Then he could reach around and feel Jason's powerful shoulders, admire the bunch and coiled strength of them as he held himself up on his arms while he ploughed his cock into Seb.

Lost in imagining, Seb only realised Will was speaking to him when he cleared his throat and said loudly, "Um. Excuse me... Mr Radcliffe?" Standing near Seb with paint-stained hands, Will looked embarrassed. He glanced over his shoulder at Jason as though following the line of Seb's focus.

Seb flushed, feeling like a child who'd been caught with his hand in the biscuit tin. "Sorry, Will. I was miles away. And please call me Seb." Seb had asked him this every time they'd interacted, but Will still insisted on being formal with him. "What's up?"

"I'm going to make some tea. Do you want anything?"

There was a kettle set up in the kitchen now, and Seb provided teabags and instant coffee, along with a generous supply of biscuits for Jason and Will.

"Tea please, thanks, Will." Seb preferred coffee but instant was disgusting. He couldn't wait until he had his own coffee machine set up and working. In the meantime, tea was preferable to Nescafé. If he craved coffee he still went out to Seaview Café to get a decent latte.

"Okay."

Once Will's back was turned, Seb allowed himself to watch Jason again, only looking away when Jason finished a section of wall and turned to put his roller down.

"This colour looks good," Jason said.

Glancing back up, Seb took the time to admire the walls instead of the man putting paint on them. They did look lovely. "Yeah. I'm happy with it."

"At first I thought it would be too dark, but it's drying a little paler than it looks on the tin."

"I like the warmth of it; it will be really cosy in the evening." Seb stood and went over to stand beside Jason, aware of the distance that was still between them. It was so hard not acknowledging there was anything more to their relationship than the professional, but after Tuesday Seb was determined not to do anything to scare Jason off.

When Jason lowered his voice and asked quietly, "Still on for tonight?" Seb whipped his head around, surprised Jason had mentioned it with Will in the next room.

"I am if you are."

Jason nodded, a smile tugging at the edges of his lips. "Definitely." There was a warmth to his gaze that sent a thrill through Seb. "Been looking forward to it."

"Me too."

Their brief exchange was cut off when Will came out of the kitchen, a mug in each hand. "That's yours, boss." He put one down near Jason. "And this one's yours, Mr Rad—Seb, I mean." He flushed, holding out the mug to Seb, handle first.

"Thanks, Will." Seb was touched that he'd remembered

to make his tea weaker than he and Jason had it. "That's just how I like it."

Will gave a shy smile before turning back to fetch his own from the kitchen.

"It's only taken him nearly three weeks to use your first name," Jason said quietly, amused.

"I know, bless him. Lord knows what he makes of me."

"He thinks you're a 'decent bloke for a poofter.' Or so he told me."

Seb whipped his head around to gauge Jason's mood but his face gave nothing away. Seb didn't care about Will calling him a poofter; he'd been called worse in his time and it sounded as though Will had been using it as a clumsy descriptor rather than a slur. But how would it make Jason feel hearing that word, knowing it applied to him too? Seb didn't have time to ask him how he felt before Will returned.

"Right, back to work," Jason said briskly, picking up his roller again while his tea cooled on the table.

WHEN JASON ARRIVED at Seb's that evening, Seb kissed him fiercely as soon as he got through the door. Seb wasn't in the mood for talking. Desperate to get Jason's cock inside him, Seb only broke the kiss to lead Jason upstairs, holding his hand tightly as they climbed.

In Seb's bedroom, he pushed Jason down onto the bed and straddled him, grinding their hardening dicks together as he kissed him again. Seb detoured to Jason's neck, breathing in his masculine scent while Jason grabbed Seb's hips and thrust up against him. "You're impatient tonight. I haven't seen you take charge like this before."

Seb drew back to see his face. "Is it okay?"

"Yeah." Jason grinned. "It's hot. What do you want to do with me?"

"I want to get us both naked, suck your cock, and then ride you. Does that sound good?"

"It sounds fucking perfect."

Sitting upright, Seb peeled off his T-shirt, enjoying Jason's admiring gaze on his torso. Seb didn't love his body, but when Jason looked at him like that he felt sexy and desirable. He climbed off Jason so they could both get undressed, and then he straddled him again, looking down at Jason's muscular torso. "You're so gorgeous." He sighed, just managing to hold back the words, *What do you see in me?* Insecurity was never sexy.

But maybe Jason sensed what Seb didn't voice, because he ran his hands up and over Seb's chest and curled a hand around the back of his neck and pulled him down. Nose-to-nose, he whispered, "I think you're gorgeous too. I love that you're smaller than me, and I love that your chest is so smooth." Then he kissed Seb, and Seb kissed him back gratefully for saying exactly what Seb had needed to hear.

Jason's cock was thick and hard and he thrust against Seb's, which had softened a little along with his attack of inadequacy. With Jason's kisses and the increasingly urgent pressure of his dick, Seb was soon back to full-mast. Hungry for Jason's cock, he broke the kiss to shuffle backwards. Spreading his legs to make space for him, Jason took his dick in his hand and held it up for Seb. "You want this?"

"Mmmm." Seb nuzzled Jason's balls, loving the scent of them. He kissed Jason's fingers one by one, then licked teasingly up the exposed shaft and dropped a kiss on the tip.

"Tease," Jason said, but he was smiling.

"Mmmm." Seb grinned too, rubbing his cheek against Jason's cock like a cat.

Picking up on his hint, Jason gripped his cock and tapped Seb's face with it. "You like that? My cock on your face?"

"Yeah." Breathless with arousal, Seb's own cock ached as Jason slowly rubbed his cockhead over Seb's lips and clean-shaven cheeks. He left a smear of precome behind and Seb licked it off his lips.

"Such a dirty boy. Do you like facials?"

Just the thought of it sent a jolt of arousal through Seb. "Yes." The idea of Jason standing over him, shooting on his face, was incredible.

"You want it in your mouth now?"

"Yes please."

Jason pushed the blunt head against Seb's lips and Seb opened for him, tasting his wetness, and moaning as Jason arched his hips and pushed in deep, cock bumping the back of Seb's throat before he drew back. Taking over the movement, Seb went to town, holding Jason's hips down and sucking him with long, slow pulls of his mouth. When he'd had his fill, he pulled off and looked at Jason's flushed cheeks. "You ready for me to ride you?"

"Fuck, yes."

"Stay there." Seb got lube and a condom from the drawer. He rolled the condom onto Jason, and then lubed his arse with the tips of two fingers. Straddling Jason, Seb took charge, positioning Jason's cock just right and easing down onto it. The stretch made him gasp and he paused, breathing hard, eyes squeezed shut.

"Jesus, Seb. You look amazing like that."

Opening his eyes, Seb's gaze locked with Jason's. Trusting his body to handle it, Seb lowered himself a little more, inching down slowly while they stared into each other's eyes until their bodies were fully joined. Jason stayed utterly still, letting Seb be in complete control. Only the tension in his muscles gave away how much it cost him. The full stretch of Jason's cock was glorious, almost too much but not, and as Seb started to ride him it was even better. His own dick bobbed, hard and aching, so he lowered his body, taking his weight on his arms. In this position he could rock back, his cock trapped between them. "That good for you?"

"Amazing."

They carried on like that for a little while, but Seb's thighs started to burn. "Can we swap places?"

"Of course."

A quick rearrangement had Seb on his back and Jason on top like in Seb's fantasy from earlier. As Jason lowered himself over Seb and slid back in with one firm thrust, Seb groaned, running his hands over Jason's back. "Yeah. Fuck me hard."

Jason obliged, ramming into Seb over and over, the rhythmic creaking of the bed in counterpoint to the slap of sweaty skin-on-skin and their breathless moans and grunts.

"Can you come soon?" Jason gasped.

"You want me to?"

"Yeah. I'm close. Want you to come first."

"Let me stroke my cock." Seb pushed at Jason's chest, getting him to lift up a little so he could get his hand between them. "There. Oh fuck, this won't take long."

Propped up on straight arms, muscles taut, Jason watched Seb's hand as he stroked himself. "Yeah." He fucked Seb harder, faster. "Wanna see you come."

"I want to see you come too," Seb said breathlessly. "Pull out and come on me when you're ready?"

"Jesus. Okay. But I'm not sure I can hold out much longer."

"I'm nearly there." Seb stroked himself faster as Jason slammed into him relentlessly. "Oh fuck, yes." He came in a blinding rush of ecstasy, body tightening around Jason's cock as he pulsed and shot all over his stomach and chest.

And then Jason was pulling out, desperately tearing off the condom and moving up to straddle Seb's chest before gripping his cock and jerking himself off. Seb moaned along with Jason at the first hot splash on his neck and chin. He closed his eyes just in time before the second spurt painted his face. Seb licked his lips, tasting Jason's release. "You done?" he asked.

"Yeah." Jason gave a huff of laughter. "Sorry, did I get you in the eye?"

"Not quite, despite your best attempt. I have good reflexes." Seb opened the one eye that wasn't pasted shut with come. "But I could use a tissue now please."

Jason climbed off him and passed him one to clean up with.

De-gunked, Seb got under the covers and lay on his side, hoping Jason might stay for a while this time. He was determined not to say anything to ruin it this time. They'd established the ground rules for this 'relationship' such as it was, and there was no need for any more discussion about boundaries. But that didn't mean they couldn't enjoy the post-sex glow together.

Jason joined him in the bed, and when he lay on his back and pulled Seb into his arms, his head on Jason's chest, Seb's heart swelled a little. He'd never been very good at separating sex from emotions, which could be a curse at times like this. His feelings for Jason already ran deeper than sexual attraction, and he was afraid of being hurt.

They lay in silence for a while, until Jason said, "I love how kinky you are."

"I'm not *that* kinky," Seb said, surprised. "I'm not into bondage, or pain, or anything like that."

"But you like come on your face. And you liked me taking charge last time, although this time you were mostly the one in control—even though I topped."

"I like the power play of sex I suppose, and it's fun to switch that around. Sometimes I like to be bossed around and used and told what to do, but sometimes I like to do the bossing."

There was a pause before Jason asked, "Do you ever top?"

"Yes. Sometimes. If I'm with a guy who wants that. I guess bottom is my default setting. But sometimes it's fun to swap. Do you ever bottom?"

Another pause. "I haven't... yet."

The shock of surprise made Seb's eyes widen. Glad Jason couldn't see his reaction, he asked carefully, "Do you want to try it?" Because damn, Seb might love being fucked, but if Jason wanted Seb to be the one to fuck him for the first time then Seb would be all over that opportunity.

"Maybe."

"With me?" The idea of Jason trusting Seb enough to do that was overwhelming. It gave Seb hope that maybe this was more than just casual, convenient sex for Jason too. Because if not, why would he ask this of Seb? He couldn't be short of options on the hook-up apps.

"Maybe." Jason tightened his arms around Seb and buried his face in Seb's hair. "If you'd want to."

"I'd be happy to," Seb said seriously. He hugged Jason more tightly too. There was so much he wanted to ask, and say, but he was afraid of breaking this connection between them. "Just let me know when... if you're up for it."

"I'll think about it."

They lay in silence a little longer. Seb's head was whirling with thoughts and hopes. The connection between them was tangible and real and he was sure Jason felt it too.

Hoping he wasn't making a horrible mistake, Seb asked, "Are you free on Saturday night?"

"Yes. Why? Do you want to get together again?" The cheerful excitement in Jason's voice gave Seb hope. "Well, yes.... But I actually have Penny and Trude coming over for dinner and was wondering whether you'd like to join us?"

A few seconds passed.

"Just as a friend?" Jason's tone was cautious.

Heart beating fast, Seb gently untangled himself from Jason's embrace so he could see his expression. "Well I wasn't planning on blowing you on the dining table while they watch." Jason's lips quirked at that. "But actually Penny guessed there was something going on, so they sort of know...."

"About us?"

"Yeah. I promise I didn't tell. I wouldn't! But Penny knew I fancied you before anything happened, and then the night after we first hooked-up she worked it out. But they know you're discreet. Neither of them would ever out you."

Jason let out a breath, his brows drawn down, but then his face relaxed again and the shadow passed. Meeting Seb's gaze he said, "Okay then."

"You're not freaked out?"

"No. Not really. And yes, I'd like to come to dinner."

A rush of happy excitement filled Seb. "Really?" He beamed. "That's awesome."

TEN

Jason was surprised by his reaction to the knowledge that Penny and Trude knew about him and Seb. He would have expected to feel more threatened by it. But it helped that as an LGBT couple themselves, he believed they would never betray his secret. More than that though, he didn't feel any different for them knowing. There was none of the vague shame or discomfort he'd been expecting.

He wondered whether he'd made a mistake in agreeing to the dinner invitation. This thing with Seb was supposed to be casual and discreet, and having dinner as a couple— albeit with a lesbian couple in the privacy of Seb's home— seemed to be raising the bar to something more than casual. But Jason couldn't regret it. In fact he found himself looking forward to it on Saturday.

Without Zoe this weekend, and without work, Jason had the whole day to himself. He took the time to do some work in the small garden at the back of his house, and then later he went out for a run along the coast path to the lighthouse and back. Running always gave him some thinking time, the regular pounding of his feet allowing his brain to settle and mull over things that were demanding his attention.

As he ran, the conversation they'd had about Seb topping him replayed in his head.

It wasn't something Jason had planned to discuss, but when it came up in conversation he realised it was something he might want to try. Since he'd started hooking up with guys, he'd always topped. He felt comfortable in that role and was totally satisfied by it, but he'd always wondered how it would feel to be on the receiving end. Until now, that wondering had always been vague and theoretical. Jason knew it should be good physically, he'd seen enough guys moaning with his dick inside them to know that being fucked by someone who knew what they were doing felt good for most men. Jason's hesitance was more about how it would make him feel emotionally. He knew it was internalised homophobia, and probably sexism as well, and he wasn't proud of it, but he couldn't help having a knee-jerk *no* reaction to the idea of "taking it up the arse," of "being the girl," or countless other stupid offensive ways that people described bottoming that implied it was some kind of weakness, something to be ashamed of.

The path turned steeper now, sloping up towards the lighthouse. Jason pushed himself harder, lungs burning, and legs aching.

With Seb, Jason reckoned he might be able to push those kinds of thoughts aside. Last time they'd fucked, Seb might have been the bottom but he'd been the one calling the shots. There was nothing about Seb that was weak, and not a hint of shame in his obvious enjoyment of being fucked by Jason. It made Jason want to try it for himself, and he trusted Seb to take care of him and make sure he enjoyed it.

Finally reaching the lighthouse out on the headland, Jason stopped to catch his breath and stretch. The weather was mixed today, breezy and brisk with fast-moving clouds breaking up the sunshine. Currently in a patch of sun, Jason shaded his eyes to admire the view after he'd stretched out his legs. Choppy waves broke on the rocks below making white foam, and a patch of shadow from a cloud scudded over the surface of the water, darkening the blue. Jason was filled with lightness, his spirits lifting and circling with the gulls overhead. With a dinner date for the evening, and the promise of more time with Seb, Jason's life felt richer than it had a few short weeks ago. Without Jason noticing, Seb had gently eased his way into Jason's affections. That realisation shot a vein of anxiety through Jason's happiness, because it meant he had some hard decisions to make if he wanted to keep Seb in his life.

Cooling fast with his sweat drying in the wind, Jason turned away and headed back down the path at a more leisurely pace.

LATER THAT AFTERNOON, Jason popped out to the nearest shop to buy milk. When he spotted copies of *Cornwall Gazette* stacked up by the counter, it reminded him that Seb's press release had gone out yesterday, so he picked a paper up and paid for that too.

Back home, he put the kettle on and started scanning the paper while he waited for it to boil. He found the article on page five, the headline large enough to jump out at him: *Gay Café to open in Porthladock.*

Jason had overheard enough of Seb and Trude's planning meeting to know they wouldn't be too happy with that as an opener. Seb wanted the café to be inclusive and preferred the umbrella acronym of LGBT or the adjective queer. But typically the local paper had kept it simple and attention-grabbing.

He poured water on his teabag and carried on reading while he stirred. The content of the article seemed okay, thankfully. Mostly laying out Seb's plans accurately as far as Jason could tell. The report ended with:

With Rainbow Place due to open in two weeks, only time will tell whether this unusual venture will be a success or not. Will it be welcomed by the local community? We'd like to hear your opinions. Have your say by emailing us for the letters page, or comment on this article on our website.

Jason took his teabag out and added milk. It had ended up a bit strong because he'd been distracted by reading. Carrying his tea to the kitchen table, he sat and opened his laptop. He didn't want to look because he was afraid of what he might see, but he had to know. Shoulders tight with tension, he navigated to the *Cornwall Gazette* website. A quick search pulled up the online version of the article and Jason scrolled down to the comments.

What a stupid idea. It's bound to close within weeks.

It's about time we had more for LGBT people round here. I hope it does well.

Why do we need it anyway? It's not like gay people can't go to other cafés and bars and stuff. And what is it with gay people wanting to shove their choices in other people's faces? Just get on with your life and stop shouting about it.

It's a cool idea having a safe space for queer people and their friends. I'm gay, and don't always feel safe in regular pubs. Me and my friends would definitely come here.

I wouldn't eat there. Who knows what you might catch? And don't bend over in the toilets.

Jason slammed the lid of his laptop shut, blood roaring

in his ears. Fucking ignorant twats. He shouldn't have looked. Stomach churning, he picked up his tea and went into the living room. He turned on the TV, desperate for distraction from the uncomfortable thoughts and feelings the negative comments had stirred up. Anger warred with shame and the moving images and voices coming from the television did nothing to calm Jason.

Why am I ashamed?

The simple and obvious answer was that Jason had grown up with his dad's casual homophobia. The "don't bend over" comment was exactly the sort of bad-taste joke that Jason had heard over and over from him. That had planted the idea that being gay was wrong, dirty, shameful, and a source of amusement to other people—especially other men. Although when Jason had grown up he'd consciously rejected his dad's values long before he'd realised that *he* was gay, subconsciously that seed of shame still lingered.

Examining that most hated of emotions, Jason realised it was multi-faceted. Deep down he still carried some shame about being gay. He'd tried hard to break free of that, but it was still there, rooted inside him. Overlaid with that was shame *about* the shame. He knew it was wrong to feel the way he did, it made him as bad as the homophobic wankers leaving their shitty comments in the paper. But his disapproval and negativity was turned inwards, eating away at him constantly. Most of all, Jason was ashamed of himself for hiding, for being a coward, for not standing up to people for fear of revealing his secret.

Jason lay on his back on the sofa and stared at the ceiling.

There was only one way out of this prison of self-loathing he'd walled himself into. The escape route was clear and obvious, light shining through a chink in the stones. All he had to do was dismantle the barrier and step out. But would the light on the other side be bright and welcoming? Or would it be a harsh searchlight that trapped him in a new way, exposed and vulnerable with nowhere to retreat?

STILL IN A PENSIVE MOOD, Jason turned up at Seb's place with a bottle of white wine in his hand.

Seb answered the door with a delighted smile. "You came."

"Did you think I wouldn't?" Jason stepped inside, waiting for Seb to close the door before he kissed him.

"Not really. Well... I didn't think you'd stand me up. But I wondered whether you might change your mind and duck out."

"I was looking forward to it." It was true, he had been earlier. Although since his emotional crisis that afternoon, Jason had been feeling less enthusiastic about socialising. He'd like to have talked to Seb about some of the things that were going on in his head, but he wouldn't be able to do that with Penny and Trude there.

"Thanks," Seb said as he took the bottle of wine Jason offered him. "Oh and it's chilled too, perfect. I'll open it now."

"I hope it's okay. I'm not a wine expert."

"I'm sure it'll be lovely, and it should go well with the chicken. Come through and I'll pour us both a glass, unless you'd rather have something else?"

Jason would rather have had beer, but wine seemed more fitting. "No, wine's great, thanks."

He followed Seb into the kitchen. It was linked to what

must previously have been a separate room by an archway. A table there was laid for four, and double doors looked out onto a small garden. It was warm in the kitchen, and a delicious smell emanated from the oven. Seb handed Jason a large glass of wine and poured one for himself.

"Cheers." He raised his glass.

Jason matched the gesture and they both drank.

The sound of the doorbell sent Seb hurrying to let in his other guests. Jason took a deep breath, preparing himself. He knew them both a little already, but it felt very different seeing them in this context.

"Jason, how lovely." Penny swooped in and kissed him on the cheek. Her curly red hair was loose and wild, and her long floral dress was very different to her work attire.

Trude greeted Jason with a firm handshake and a warm smile. She was dressed simply in jeans, flip-flops, and a white T-shirt that stood out against her dark skin. "Hi, Jason. Good to see you again."

"You too." He took another gulp of his wine.

Seb moved in next to Jason where he leaned against the kitchen counter. "This is nice. All my favourite Porthladock people in one place. Thank you all for coming." He slipped his arm around Jason's waist.

Jason stiffened and fought the urge to jerk away. *It's okay. They know, and it's fine.* With concentrated effort, he relaxed against Seb, and put a reciprocal arm around his shoulders.

"Are you having a good weekend so far?" Seb asked Penny and Trude.

"Yes, thanks. We both promised each other we wouldn't do any work." Trude glanced sideways at Penny who smiled. "So we've been doing lovely relaxing things instead. We went for a walk down near Gorran Haven this morning, and then we took Carson up to the north coast this afternoon. He wanted to do some body boarding, and we chilled out on the beach."

"It wasn't warm though," Seb said. "Weren't you freezing?"

"Doesn't need to be warm to be fun. We had a windbreak, a flask of tea, some cake, and a blanket to snuggle under." Penny took Trude's hand and laced their fingers together. "It was quite romantic."

"Until Carson came back and told us off for snogging, and then accidentally kicked sand all over the cake." Trude chuckled, and then added to Jason, "Carson's our son by the way."

"How old is he?" Jason asked.

"Fourteen."

"Oh. I have a twelve-year-old daughter. Is he at Porthladock High?"

"Yes. In year nine."

"Zoe's year seven so they probably don't know each other." Jason realised Seb was rather left out of this conversation. Talking about the daughter Seb hadn't even seen yet, let alone met, was a little awkward. He changed the subject quickly. "Whatever you have in the oven smells amazing, Seb. What is it?"

"Pesto stuffed chicken wrapped in prosciutto, and roasted vegetables with couscous."

"Wow." Jason started drooling at the thought.

"In fact"—Seb turned to check the timer on the oven—"it's almost ready. Why don't you guys take a seat and I'll do the last-minute prep."

"Can we help with anything?" Penny offered.

"You know what they say about too many cooks. Sit and drink your wine, everything's under control."

Jason let Penny and Trude go through the archway first. He was about to follow, when Seb said, "Actually, I could do with one extra pair of hands. Jason, can I keep you?"

His turn of phrase and teasing smile made Jason flush and grin back. "What do you want me to do?"

"Hang on." Seb put oven gloves on and got a baking dish out of the oven. He put it down on the counter and handed Jason a serving spoon. "Scoop these into that bowl of couscous and stir them in while I check the chicken. Sorry, I only have one pair of oven gloves." He handed Jason a folded tea towel.

Feeling very much like one half of a couple, Jason busied himself with helping. Seb came to check the mixture, putting a casual hand in the small of Jason's back while he did so. The light touch sent a tingle up Jason's spine and made warmth rise in his chest. He liked the domesticity. It made him imagine other non-sexual things they might do together if they were a real couple, like going for a walk or eating out in a restaurant together.

By the time they got everything ready and to the table, Jason's stomach was rumbling with hunger. Everything looked incredible and he was glad to see there was plenty of it. Seb sipped his wine, insisting the others helped themselves first. Jason let Penny and Trude dig in, relieved that Trude took a good-sized portion so he didn't feel too bad when he loaded his plate.

"Please start, don't let it get cold." Seb started serving himself, and the others began eating.

"Mmm," Penny exclaimed. "This is incredible, Seb. Where did you get the recipe?"

"I didn't. It's one of the dishes that Luca—the chef I've just hired—suggested for the evening menu. It sounded pretty straightforward so I made up this version."

"Seriously?" Jason was impressed. "You're an amazing cook."

Seb flushed, looking pleased. "I've always loved food." He patted his flat stomach. "So there was plenty of motivation to learn. I just have to make sure I don't pig out on the results."

Trude snorted. "There's not much danger of that."

"You haven't seen what I've made for pudding yet." Seb grinned.

"Well if you serve food like this in Rainbow Place, you should get rave reviews from the food critics," Penny said. "How is the initial PR going? We've been out all day so didn't have time to check the papers—plus Trude is on a work ban of course, but I'm asking because I know she'll be desperate to know." Penny glanced at Trude, her gaze warm with affection.

Trude smiled. "I must confess, I've been resisting the urge to sneak off to the toilet to look at my phone."

"Most of the local papers and news sites have used the story. They didn't change the content much but some of the headlines were a little different to ours," Seb said.

"And the response so far?" Trude asked.

Jason's stomach clenched, the food in his mouth suddenly losing flavour as he remembered some of the nasty comments he'd been trying to forget.

Seb wrinkled his nose and shrugged. "Mixed, as you'd expect. But nothing too awful."

If he didn't find those comments awful, Jason wondered what Seb had been braced for.

"Well that's good," Trude said. "And remember, even if there is backlash it's all publicity, and any extra exposure from the haters is only going to help your target audience find out about what you're doing."

"Absolutely." Seb raised his glass. "Here's to pissing off the homophobes."

Chuckling, Penny and Trude joined the toast. Jason raised his glass too, admiring their nonchalance in the face of such personal negativity, but he couldn't bring himself to smile with the rest of them. As he put his glass down, he caught Seb watching him, a line of concern on his forehead.

IT WAS A LOVELY EVENING. They finished two bottles of wine between them and made in-roads into a third. The pudding—chocolate torte with strawberries and clotted cream—was divine. After dinner they moved through to Seb's cosy living room where he lit candles and poured them brandies.

"I need to get around to buying a lamp for in here. The overhead one is horribly glaring."

"The candlelight is lovely though," Penny said.

"It is," Trude agreed.

She and Penny were sitting cuddled up together on one of the two-seater sofas. Penny had kicked off her sandals and had her feet tucked up where she leaned against Trude.

When Seb had finished handing out the drinks, he joined Jason on the other sofa, sitting close, and putting a hand on Jason's thigh. Jason put his arm around Seb, letting him settle into his side. They fit perfectly like this and the weight of Seb against him warmed Jason from the inside out.

The conversation drifted idly. Mostly listening rather than participating, Jason's head was a little fuzzy from alcohol. He marvelled at how they flitted from topic to topic. Food, politics, education, and somehow back to food again.

"I want the recipe for that chocolate torte," Penny was saying.

"I'll e—" Seb broke off, yawning hugely "—email it to you tomorrow."

"Thanks." Penny yawned too. "Oh God, it's catching. I think that's probably our cue to depart." She untangled herself from Trude and stood, offering Trude a hand up. "No, don't bother to move," she said as Seb started to push himself up from the sofa. "We can let ourselves out." She came to Seb and stooped to give him a hug and a kiss, and then moved along to Jason, kissing him too. This time Trude also gave Jason a kiss on the cheek.

"It was lovely to get to know you a little better, Jason," Trude said.

"Yes. Perhaps the two of you would like to come to ours one night?" Penny smiled at them both.

"That sounds like a nice idea." Seb squeezed Jason's thigh where his hand lay on it.

"Yeah, thanks." Jason was touched to be included in this plan, but felt a frisson of anxiety at what he was getting himself into. Double dinner dates was serious stuff, a far cry from the uncomplicated sex he'd been hoping for when he'd first hooked-up with Seb. But hopes could change, just like people could change. Jason felt a shift in himself like the sea being pulled by the moon. Seb made him want different things, showing him a glimpse of a future Jason had never allowed himself to consider before.

As the front door clicked shut leaving them alone at last, Seb turned in Jason's arms and pressed a kiss to his cheek. Jason moved to meet him and kissed Seb on the lips. "That was a great evening. Thanks for inviting me."

"I'm glad you wanted to come." Seb kissed him again, deeper this time. Not wanting to break the kiss, Jason pulled

Seb into his lap so they could face each other. He wrapped his arms around Seb and held him close while Seb slid his fingers into Jason's hair. They stayed like that for a while, lazy arousal building but without the urgency to take it any further. Jason's mind and body were exhausted from a busy week, and the alcohol in his veins made him crave affection more than sexual release. Seb seemed to be in the same place, because he didn't push for more.

Their kisses gradually slowed, and after a final brush of his mouth on Jason's lips, Seb kissed Jason on the cheek, and then buried his face in his neck, arms looped around Jason's shoulders. His breath was warm and ticklish. "This is nice," he said quietly.

"Yes." Jason tightened his hold on Seb.

Time seemed to stand still as Jason lost himself in the weight of Seb on his lap, the warmth of his embrace, the slowing rasp of his breath. He felt his own heartrate slow, and sleepiness began to weight his limbs. A few minutes later, maybe more, Jason said quietly, "Seb?"

No reply.

"Seb." Jason squeezed him gently.

"Huh? Oh!" Seb raised his head with an apologetic smile. "Sorry. I'm literally falling asleep on you. It's nothing personal, I promise, wine makes me sleepy."

"It's okay. I was almost dropping off myself. I should probably head home and let you get to bed."

Seb held his gaze for a moment, searching Jason's face for something, and then he said, "You can stay here if you like."

Jason felt tension stiffen Seb's muscles as he asked the question. His heart tripped, beating faster as he considered Seb's offer. Suddenly wide awake again, he was torn in two directions. It was so tempting to say yes. To go upstairs with

Seb and sleep together, wake together, maybe have some lazy morning sex, then breakfast.... Jason desperately wanted all those things, but with the negative comments nagging at the back of his mind, he wasn't sure how well he'd be able to sleep. Plus staying the night would definitely push their relationship to a new level of intimacy. Jason wasn't sure he was ready for that, not yet.

"Thanks.... But I think it would be best if I went home tonight."

"Okay. No worries. I guess we'll both get a better night's sleep if we're alone anyway." Seb's disappointment was obvious, although he tried valiantly to hide it.

"Yeah, I snore sometimes, especially after booze." Jason tried to lighten the mood.

"And I steal the covers." A small smile lifted Seb's lips. He climbed off Jason and offered him a hand, pulling him up. "I'll see you out then."

By the front door, Jason kissed Seb thoroughly, trying to pour the apology he felt he owed Seb but couldn't find words for into the embrace. When he finally released Seb he asked, "Want to set a date for next week?"

Seb's smile was brighter again this time. "Yes."

"I can do any evening apart from Wednesday, and then I have Zoe again at the weekend."

"Tuesday?"

"Perfect."

ELEVEN

On Monday morning Seb was in good spirits.

He'd bounced back from his disappointment at Jason choosing not to stay over on Saturday night. In retrospect he probably shouldn't have asked him. He'd already gone out on a limb asking Jason to dinner with Penny and Trude. He had to keep reminding himself that Jason was in the closet and not looking for a serious relationship. Seb needed to enjoy things for what they were and make sure he didn't scare Jason away by being too pushy.

Before going to Rainbow Place he made a detour to Seaview Café.

"Good morning," he greeted Janine, the lady who ran the place with her husband, Andrew. "Can I order my usual to take away please, along with two cups of tea?"

"Of course, love." She smiled at him and wrote down the order, passing it to a young man who was busy at the coffee machine before coming back to Seb, taking the ten-pound note he offered and ringing the order up. "I saw the article about your place in the paper. That's a bold move." She handed him his change.

Searching her face for negativity, Seb saw only genuine interest. "I'm sure some people will think it's crazy. But I wanted to try to do something unique."

"Well it's certainly that! You've caused quite a stir. We were down having a drink at The Anchor on Saturday night, and you're the talk of the town."

"Oh?" Seb raised his eyebrows. "Is that a good thing or a bad thing?"

"Bit of both I reckon. You're bound to get some people who don't like it, but good for you I say. Live and let live."

The young man came over with the tray of drinks and put them in front of Seb. "I think it's cool," he said. "My brother's gay. He doesn't live here anymore, he moved to Exeter, but I'll buy him a coffee at your new place next time he comes to visit." He gave Seb a shy smile.

"Thanks." Seb was touched.

"I hope it works out for you, love," Janine said. "Best of luck with it."

As he thanked her, Seb wondered if part of her enthusiasm was that she no longer saw him as much competition. Maybe she thought he'd need all the luck he could get.

Slightly deflated, he walked back with the tray of drinks. The door to Rainbow Place was already standing open when he arrived. Jason had a key, so he and Will must have already started for the day. He wondered whether Will had seen or heard the news, and how he felt about it. He hoped it wouldn't cause problems. If Will had issues with it, that would put Jason in a very tricky position.

"Morning," Seb said brightly as he walked in. His cheerful tone belied the worries that were nagging at him. Was he stupid to try to create such a niche in a small town, in a county that wasn't known for its diversity?

"Hi," Jason replied from up a ladder where he was

painting the top edge of a wall. He looked over his shoulder and smiled. There was no sign of Will.

"Will not in yet?" Seb said hopefully. A few minutes alone with Jason might be nice, just to talk without the need to be guarded.

"He's in the toilet."

"Oh, right. I brought you some tea. I was getting coffee for me, so...." Seb put the tray down on a table.

"Cheers. We hadn't got around to making any here yet so that's perfect timing." Jason climbed down from the ladder. "Which is mine?"

Seb slid one of the cups towards him. "Has Will said anything about the news?"

"No." Jason's expression was neutral. Seb wondered if he was hiding his anxiety too. "I'm not sure if he's heard yet."

"Do you want me to tell him?"

A shrug. "Maybe? If you think that's best."

The flush of the toilet and the sound of Will's heavy tread put a stop to their conversation.

"Good morning, Will, how was your weekend?" Seb asked.

"Hiya, good thanks. Yours?"

"Very nice, thank you." Seb carefully avoided catching Jason's eye. Presumably he wouldn't have mentioned their Saturday night dinner to Will. "I brought you some tea."

"Oh, ta." Will favoured Seb with a rare smile.

Deciding to bite the bullet, and hoping Will wasn't going to be a dick about it, Seb said, "I was wondering if you'd heard the news about the café? The theme of it? There was something about it in the papers this weekend so you might have seen it."

Will glanced up from his tea again. "I didn't see it, but

one of my mates mentioned it in the pub." He sounded unconcerned, so Seb relaxed a little.

"Um. Did he have much to say about it?"

"My mate? He thought it was a bit weird, and asked me if I was bothered about it." Will shrugged. "I told him I didn't care as long as you paid me. Then he asked me what you were like and I told him you were sound."

Seb held back a smile at that. "Well thanks."

"Right. I'd best get on." Will put his tea down and picked up a paintbrush.

"Me too." Encouraged by Will's equanimity, Seb moved his coffee to his current workstation—he kept moving tables to stay away from the decorating—and got out his laptop. Determined to stay away from the comments on the blogs, his job today was to set up a Facebook page, Instagram, and Twitter for Rainbow Place now the name had been announced and the publicity was in full swing. He was also due to meet with Luca and Amelia later to finalise the menus so they could put them on the website soon.

FOR THE NEXT couple of days, things ticked along happily. Work in the café was progressing well, and the big excitement on Tuesday morning was the delivery of the coffee machine and fridges. The cookers were the last big appliances to be installed and they were due on Friday.

Aside from a few more negative comments online—Seb couldn't help checking occasionally—the response was mostly either positive or neutral. A few local shop owners dropped by to take a look at the place and talk to Seb about his plans. He got the impression that some of them were humouring him, clearly thinking it was going to flop, but others were warmly supportive.

"I think it's wonderful," Laura said. She was the owner of a shop that sold crystals and jewellery, and displayed work from local artists. "It's such a positive thing to be doing. Good for you." She hugged him impulsively with a jangle of bracelets and a waft of patchouli oil.

"Thank you." Seb detached himself, touched by her enthusiasm.

TUESDAY EVENING with Jason was blissful again. The sex was as good as ever, and afterwards Jason stayed for a while. They lay in bed in an intimate tangle of limbs sharing lazy caresses and talking. They started off discussing the café, but somehow the conversation drifted to Seb's history and what had made him decide to move to Cornwall.

Seb glossed over the more painful details of his break up, just saying he'd parted ways with someone he'd been with for over a year. Jason didn't ask for more information and Seb was grateful. Being dumped by his younger lover for another younger man still stung, and it had knocked a huge hole in his confidence. Seb's insecurity made it difficult for him to believe he was attractive enough to hold Jason's interest, but he was reluctant to reveal his vulnerability.

Jason just said, "Well, it's his loss," and hugged Seb more tightly.

"Yeah," Seb agreed, wishing he could feel the truth in the words. Wanting to change the subject he asked, "So what about your ex? You said she's the only one who knows about you. Are you still close?"

"Yeah, Anna—my ex—is great. She's my best friend I suppose."

Seb wondered what had happened between them but

didn't want to pry. Carefully, he said, "Yes, it's good that you get on well. Must be good for your daughter too."

"It helped that Anna was the one who pushed for change. I was still deep in denial, and not ready to go looking for anything because I was scared. Our sex life was virtually non-existent but I kept using the excuse of being tired because of the baby, when actually I wasn't too tired to jerk off to gay porn on my phone before coming up to bed. Anyway once Zoe started sleeping through, Anna began talking about getting the spark back in our relationship. We tried. *I* tried, but there was no chemistry and I couldn't fake it." Jason sighed, and Seb stroked his chest.

"That sounds tough."

"Yeah. I felt guilty as hell, even though I hadn't done anything. I was so ashamed. Anna finally demanded to know what was going on, and I managed to tell her. She deserved the truth."

"How did she take it?"

"At first she was angry and hurt. But once the dust settled, she was almost relieved I think. She was glad to know that it really wasn't anything she'd done, or not done. It was all my issue."

"And she's been supportive since?"

"Yes. Always. Although she keeps nagging me to come out and start dating properly. She'd approve of you."

Seb's heartrate kicked up a notch. Were they dating properly in Jason's eyes? "Do you think so?" He kept his voice carefully casual.

"Definitely." Jason paused, and the moment was almost unbearable. Then he said, "Maybe I could introduce you to her sometime. If you like?"

"I'd love that," Seb blurted in a happy rush. "If you want to?"

"Yeah. I think I do."

Seb rolled on top of Jason and kissed him, trying not to let the hope in his chest spread its wings too wide in case he couldn't contain it.

THE BOMBSHELL CAME EARLY on Wednesday, with a phone call from Trude first thing while Seb was still making his morning coffee.

"What's up?" he asked sleepily.

"Nothing good I'm afraid," she replied. Her grim tone woke Seb up more effectively than caffeine could. "There's a really nasty letter about Rainbow Place in the local news this morning. I've emailed you the link."

Seb's stomach dropped as though it was filled with cement. "How bad is it?" Forgetting his coffee brewing, he hurried to open his laptop and power it up.

"It's pretty bad."

"Who wrote the letter?" Seb tapped his fingers impatiently, waiting for his laptop to start.

"A bloke called Martin Elliot. He's a right wanker, but an influential one unfortunately for us. He owns a couple of big holiday parks and invests in various other local businesses, has his fingers in a lot of pies down here. He has political connections too. Before Brexit he was the UKIP candidate down here, and now he's smarming up to the local Tory MP."

"He sounds like a right charmer." Seb had got into his emails now and he clicked on the link from Trude. "Okay. I've got it. Reading now."

Trude went quiet while Seb scanned the letter with a sick feeling in his belly.

I'm dismayed to learn that a so-called LGBT-friendly

café is soon to open in Porthladock, and am led to question whether this is the right thing for our community, especially for vulnerable young people. Dress it up with a fancy acronym as much as you like, but to me it sounds like the homosexual agenda is being subtly, or not-so-subtly, pushed on us in the form of tea and cake. Why on earth does Porthladock need a "safe and inclusive space" for gays? This isn't 1960, they already have equal rights.

I sincerely hope the local community will vote with their feet, and that this venture will fail before it gets started.

Martin Elliot.

"For fuck's fucking sake!" Seb exploded, nausea morphing into fury.

"My thoughts exactly." Trude sounded calm, but there was an edge of ice to her voice that gave away her anger.

"What a fucking arsehole. He might as well have said 'think of the children.' Jesus Christ. With bigoted idiots like him around the local kids need us all the more." Finger hovering over his trackpad, Seb asked, "Do I even dare look at the comments?"

"This only went live half an hour ago, there's nothing there yet."

"What do we do? Do we retaliate?"

"Not yet. Let's wait and see how much attention it gets. It's possible that it will die down. But if not, then yes, I think we should respond to it. Are you free later to meet?"

"Not till much later this afternoon. I'm interviewing all day today for kitchen assistants and servers. I should be done by about three."

"Okay, I'll pop down then. Have a good day, and try not to worry too much. Even if this does create a stir, it will rally your supporters too."

"Let's hope so." Seb closed the tab on his browser. He

didn't want to see those words when he opened it up again later. "See you this afternoon. Thanks, Trude."

SEB FELT EXPOSED and vulnerable as he walked down to the café. Whenever he caught the eye of a passer-by, he wondered who else in this small town shared Martin Elliot's views. He had to hope the unpleasant twat was in a minority.

Lacking his usual morning cheer, he gave Jason and Will a muted, "Morning," as he arrived and went to set up an interview space by one of the front windows. Jason and Will were putting a second coat of paint on the walls, so they had all the doors and windows open again.

"Hi. You okay?" Jason asked, a concerned expression on his face. "You sound a bit glum."

"Shitty letter to the local news website about the café. But it's nothing we can't handle."

"Oh?" Jason put his brush down and approached. "What did it say?"

"The usual crap. Gay agenda, vulnerable young people, blah blah blah." Seb waved his hands. "It was written by some ex-UKIP bloke who obviously has nothing better to do now. Hopefully nobody will pay any attention to it."

"Oh. Martin Elliot I assume?"

"Yes."

Jason frowned. "He has a lot of clout in this town, and he's a nasty piece of work."

"Do you know him?"

"I've done some work for him in the past. He's not someone you want to get on the wrong side of."

"Yeah. He's a right git," Will agreed, without turning from his painting.

Seb gave a harsh snort of laughter. "Well it's a bit bloody late for me isn't it? I've clearly got a target on my back and I haven't even met the man." Anxiety churned in his guts, and he realised he'd forgotten to eat breakfast. Jason's frown hadn't lifted, and his attitude was doing nothing to make Seb feel better. "Anyway. I have a job to do, and so do you. No point worrying about something I can't control." He started unpacking his bag. Deliberately keeping his back to Jason, he took his time arranging his desk for the day. When he was done, Jason was back at work. "Do either of you want some tea or coffee?" Now they had the coffee machine set up, he didn't necessarily have to go out for his caffeine fix. It was a shame he didn't have time to go out and buy breakfast, but his first interviewee was due in five minutes.

"Tea please," both Will and Jason said.

THE INTERVIEWS WENT WELL. Seb was pleased to have had plenty of applicants. Most of them were young people, mainly students wanting part-time work to fit around school or college, but he had a few older candidates too. Absorbed in asking questions and making notes, Seb was mostly able to set aside his worries about the letter, but every now and then it would pop into his head and his stomach would lurch again. Even lunch didn't help settle it.

By the time he was done with interviews, it was almost time to meet Trude. Seb quickly finished his notes on the last candidate and scanned down the list of names. He was fairly sure who he was going to offer work to, but he'd make his final decision this evening.

Bracing himself, Seb opened the letter again and his heart sank as he scrolled down the alarmingly long comment thread. He didn't read every one, but it was easy to see at a glance that all the bigots had crawled out of the woodwork to agree with Martin's sentiment. Thankfully there were supporters there too, arguing their case, but the weight of negativity was depressing.

Trude arrived while he was still reading, and the expression on her face matched Seb's mood.

"I've just looked again," he said. "That comment thread isn't good."

"That's not the worst of it, though. He's been sharing it all over social media too."

"Shit."

"Yes." Trude sat down beside him and got out her laptop. "Look." She opened Facebook, and then Twitter, and showed him the responses there. As on the news site, there were people replying in support of Seb's café, but there were also lots of others agreeing with Martin's views—or worse. Social media gave a voice to haters, and they were out in force today.

Feeling sick again, Seb pushed the laptop away. "I don't want to read anymore. What do we do, Trude?"

"We fight back." She opened up a document and started to type.

An open letter to Martin Elliot.
Dear Martin

"What do you want to say to him?"

"I want to call him out for being a homophobe and a bigot, tell him how utterly stupid his views are, and then question the size of his dick."

Trude chuckled. "Okay, maybe we need to write two versions, and then you could get that out of your system first."

"No, that version has been going round in my head all

day. Let's do this properly." Seb focused on the task ahead of them. "So, maybe we could start with something like: While we recognise your concerns for the local community, we'd like to point out all the ways in which we believe Rainbow Place will benefit that community."

"Sounds good." Trude typed quickly, fingers flying over the keys.

Half an hour later, they were done. Utterly engaged in drafting and editing their response, Seb had hardly noticed Jason put two coffees and a couple of Danish pastries down on the table, but he'd drunk his anyway and demolished the pastry—though he'd barely tasted either.

Belatedly he raised his head, seeking out Jason in the far corner and called across, "Thanks! I needed that." He raised the empty cup.

"I thought you might." Jason smiled, but there was tension in his jaw and he turned quickly back to his work.

"Right, a final read-through before we send it?" Trude asked.

"Yes." Seb read the letter aloud.

"Dear Martin

"While we recognise your desire to protect the local community, we'd like to point out all the ways in which we believe Rainbow Place will benefit that community.

"LGBT people live here too, and providing a safe and inclusive space that welcomes them sends a positive message to a group who often feel marginalised or discriminated against.

"You mention the "homosexual agenda." This is simply a negative and damaging term for advocacy. As an out-and-proud gay man, I'm happy to call myself an advocate and I see that as a positive thing.

"While Rainbow Place is intended to be queer-friendly,

it will also be a welcoming space for friends, family, and allies of LGBT people. We're providing jobs for the community, and have plans to exhibit the work of local artists, and provide a performance space for musicians, singers, and poets. We want to make Rainbow Place a truly inclusive space where anyone who believes in LGBT equality is welcome.

"*Your letter also refers to "vulnerable young people," implying that what we're trying to do at Rainbow Place will somehow be damaging to them. Yet according to recent government statistics, one in every twenty young people identify as LGBT, and young queer people are one of the most vulnerable groups of all. What we're doing will help them, not harm them.*

"*Finally, you question why such a place is necessary. Yes, it may be true that gay and bisexual people may legally have the same rights as others in the UK, but trans rights are still a battleground. However, you need to remember that equality is about more than the law. Equality is about being able to walk down the street and hold the hand of your same-sex partner without being stared at—or worse. Equality is about not being exposed to attitudes like yours that make us feel as though our identity is something to be ashamed of.*

"*As long as people like you challenge the existence of safe places for queer people, then safe places for queer people will be necessary.*

"*Regards*

"*Seb Radcliffe (owner/manager of Rainbow Place)."*

There was a silence after Seb finished reading. He raised his eyes to meet Trude's and she nodded and smiled. "It's good."

"Shall I send it?" Seb asked.

"Yes." Jason's voice made them turn in surprise. Even

Will had stopped painting and was looking at Jason, eyebrows raised. "It's a great letter."

"It had a lot of long words in it," Will chimed in. "But it sounded pretty good to me too. And all that vulnerable young people stuff is bollocks. If you're gay you're gay, or bi. Whatever. Having a gay café isn't gonna turn anyone is it? Martin Elliot is a bloody idiot." That was the longest string of words Seb had ever heard from Will. By the end of his speech his face was pink. "What are you all staring at?"

Seb felt a hot rush of emotion at Will's unexpected support. "Thank you, Will. That means a lot."

Even the tips of Will's ears were red now. He ducked his head away and turned back to his painting. "Just telling it like it is."

Catching Jason's gaze, Seb stared back. There was an intensity there, and Seb wondered how it felt to Jason hearing Will's words. He hoped it gave Jason some reassurance, some confidence in the knowledge that if he did come out one day, he'd have plenty of people on his side.

"Seb." Trude's quiet voice brought him back to the present. "Are you going to send it?"

"Yes," Seb said decisively. He took a deep breath and hit send. "Now what?"

"Copy and paste it as a blog post, then copy and paste onto the Facebook page—that will automatically share to Twitter—then share the Facebook post on your personal page and ask your friends to share it too. I'll share it on mine, and so will Penny. Hopefully word will spread."

"I'll share it on mine if you want." Will surprised Seb again. "If it helps?"

"That would be amazing, Will," Trude replied before Seb could think what to say. "And if you can add your opinion too, what you said to us just now for instance, that would be even better."

"I'll give it a go. I'm not good with words like you. Am I allowed to call him a twat?"

Seb chuckled as Trude replied, "You can call him what you like on your own Facebook wall."

"Cool."

LATER THAT DAY, when Will had left and Seb was going over his list of people to call about jobs, Jason came over.

"I'm done for today."

"Okay." Seb raised his gaze, but stayed in his seat. The urge to give Jason a hug and a kiss was strong, but they'd agreed to keep things platonic in the workplace. They'd made another date for Sunday night. That felt like an awfully long time away. But Jason had Zoe tonight and at the weekend, and Seb was going to the cinema with Penny on Thursday.

"About the letter thing.... I would have offered to share it on Facebook, but I don't really use it much, so I'm not sure it would be worth it." Jason's expression was sheepish. Seb waited. "Plus I don't want to draw attention to myself over this. I'm sorry."

Ignoring the twist of disappointment, Seb shrugged. "It's okay. I get it." He couldn't blame Jason, not really. But it was also impossible to deny that his lack of support hurt even though Seb understood it.

"I'll ask Anna to share it. She's got way more Facebook friends than me anyway, and she'll definitely have something to say about Martin Elliot and his stupid letter." Jason gave Seb a hopeful smile, as though asking for forgiveness.

"Great idea. Thanks."

"I'll see you tomorrow then," Jason said, but still didn't move.

"Okay. Bye. Have a nice evening." Seb tore his gaze away and went back to his list. He made a few meaningless marks on the paper, waiting until he heard Jason turn and walk away.

When the door closed behind Jason, Seb sighed and laid his head down on the table. He banged his forehead on the wood, not enough to hurt, but wishing he could knock some sense into himself. He was in too deep with Jason, although it clearly wasn't going anywhere. It was already hurting him, small jabs like paper cuts with each bit of secrecy. Seb knew he should get out before he fell even harder, and try and save himself from being hurt worse in the future. But he was weak, and Jason was lovely, and Seb knew he wouldn't be able to break it off.

Not unless Jason gave him more of a reason to do so.

TWELVE

When Jason went to pick Zoe up, he was glad to catch Anna alone downstairs while Zoe was still packing her bag.

"I have a favour to ask you," he said.

"Oh?"

"It's more for Seb than me. You know there was stuff in the paper about the café?"

Anna nodded. "Yes, I saw the article online."

"Well, Martin Elliot's chimed in with a shitty letter which went viral."

"Ugh. Bloody typical. He's such a vile man."

"Anyway. Seb's written an open letter in response, and the more people who share it on social media the better. Would you mind sharing it on Facebook?"

"Of course not." Anna was already opening her laptop where it stood on the kitchen worktop. "How do I find it?"

"Rainbow Place has a Facebook page; you can find the post there."

A few clicks and a short burst of typing later, Anna said, "Done. I tagged a few people who I think will want to share it too."

"Thank you."

"So, things are still going okay with you and Seb then?" She turned, leaning against the counter, and smiling knowingly.

Unease rolled slowly through Jason's stomach. "Sort of." He was afraid that Seb was slipping away from him while he procrastinated. "I'm thinking about coming out," he blurted.

Anna's face lit up. "Jase, that's wonderful."

"But I'm not quite sure I'm there yet. It feels so overwhelming, Anna."

Her expression morphed into something softer. "I can only imagine."

"I'll tell Zoe first. I'm not sure when, though. Maybe quite soon. I thought I'd wait till after the opening of the café, let all the drama around this settle. I want to come out slowly, one step at a time. Zoe, my parents"—his stomach rolled at the thought of telling his dad—"Will, a few old friends...."

"You don't need to tell everyone all at once. It's not something you have to announce to the world."

"Yes, but once I start to tell people then word will spread."

"Maybe. But anyone who has a problem with it isn't someone you want to keep in your life anyway. It will be fine, Jason. I'm sure." Jason nodded, wishing he felt even a fraction of Anna's certainty. "Does Seb know what you're planning? Will it change things between you?"

"No. And I don't know. We haven't talked about what we want from each other. Although he's the catalyst, I need to be doing this for me, not for him. And I'm afraid of mentioning it to him in case I bottle it. I don't want to get his hopes up and then let him down." Jason cut himself off abruptly as he heard Zoe coming down the stairs, and then added. "I'll work it out."

Anna nodded, and gave him a reassuring smile.

"Hi, Dad." Zoe came to give Jason a hug.

He hugged her back, lifting her off her feet, and making her giggle. "How's my gorgeous girl?"

"I'm good thanks."

"Let's go then." He put her down. "See you soon," he said to Anna.

"Have a nice evening you two." Anna gave Zoe a kiss. "Bye, darling."

JASON COOKED macaroni cheese for dinner, with Zoe's help. She insisted on putting on some Korean pop music that she was currently obsessed with. Jason teased her by doing terrible dance moves while she rolled her eyes at him.

After they'd eaten, Zoe went up to her room to do some homework, and Jason sat on the sofa with a beer and turned the telly on. He channel-hopped for a while but there was nothing much that caught his attention, so he left it on a wildlife documentary and got out his phone.

Curiosity made him open the Facebook app for the first time in ages. He had a few notifications, but they were all from people he hardly knew inviting him to play games he'd never heard of, so he marked them all as read and looked at his timeline instead.

He saw Anna's post immediately. It was right at the top and read: *What a perfect response to bigotry. I will definitely be supporting Rainbow Place when it opens.*

Her post had over thirty likes and had been shared five times. Jason skimmed down the comment thread and saw a few people saying disparaging things about Martin Elliot, and supportive things about Seb's plans.

Heartened, Jason scrolled, and then blinked in surprise. The post below Anna's was the same post, shared by Zoe this time—just ten minutes ago.

Vulnerable young people my arse! This response is ace.

Jason snorted at his daughter's choice of words. He decided to ignore the fact that she'd shared the post when she was supposed to be doing her homework. Her immediate support of Rainbow Place shot Jason through with pride entwined with hope.

He let his thumb hover over the screen for a moment before hitting like on her post.

A minute later, he got a notification on Messenger.

Dad, what are you doing on Facebook? You're never on Facebook!

Jason replied with: *What are YOU doing on Facebook? You're supposed to be doing your homework.*

Fair point, Zoe replied, with the crying laughing emoji. *Okay, I'll get back to it xxx*

Scrolling his timeline again, Jason came across the link to Seb's blog post a third time. This one was Will's.

Martin Elliot is such a twat. If you're gay you're gay. Going to a gay café isn't gonna turn you.

Jason chuckled. Will's post had a few likes and a couple of comments.

Still sounds like a daft idea to me.

And the other read: *Good thing too as you've been working there for weeks. There's no hope for you if it's catching.*

Will had replied: *Sorry, mate. I'm still not into you.*

Amusement was tempered with strange conflicting feelings. Envy of Will's easy ability to turn the joke back on the commenter, and guilt that Will—and Anna, and Zoe—were lending vocal support to Seb while Jason stayed silent.

He liked Will's post too and then scrolled back up to like Anna's, but those tiny acts of solidarity weren't enough to assuage Jason's disappointment in himself.

BUSY FIXING PIECES of second-hand furniture, Jason couldn't help listening in to the conversation Seb was having a few tables away. It was Friday afternoon and Seb was being interviewed by someone from the *Gazette*. Quentin something, Jason hadn't caught his surname.

The interview had been arranged at short notice in the wake of all the controversy surrounding Rainbow Place since Martin's letter. Seb's subsequent response had been shared even more widely on social media than Martin's original letter. Everyone in town was talking about it, and even people who weren't local were sharing and commenting on the posts.

"I think it's brilliant what you're doing here," Quentin said enthusiastically. "I want to make this piece really positive. So this is your chance to give your side of the story, and hopefully get more support when people understand where you're coming from. A personal angle would be great, so I'm going to ask you about your life and experiences as well as focusing on Rainbow Place and why you wanted to open it."

Jason repositioned himself so he could see them better, glancing up from the table leg he was tightening. Quentin looked as though he should still be in school rather than out interviewing people for the local paper. He had messy dark hair and thick-rimmed glasses and was undeniably cute.

Jason also suspected he was interested in Seb for reasons other than his newsworthiness.

"Um, okay. But I'd like to get final approval on exactly what goes to print," Seb said. "I sometimes forget to stop talking when I'm nervous and if I end up oversharing there might be some things I don't want you to use." He gave a nervous chuckle.

"Absolutely, that's fine. I can show you the interview once I've written it up. Shall we make a start?"

He began by asking Seb about his past. About when he knew he was gay, and how it was for him when he started coming out to people.

"I was never very good at hiding it," Seb said. "I got called a fag at school long before I told anyone. So when I *did* tell people it was only confirming what most of them already suspected."

"Did the bullying get worse?"

"A bit. But I found some supporters too. Coming out showed me who my real friends were."

"Would it have helped you having somewhere you were accepted unconditionally? A safe space like you're trying to create here?"

"Definitely. That's why I moved to London as soon as I was old enough. I was craving community, somewhere I could connect with other people who were like me. Finding that was enormously helpful."

"And why did you decide to move away from London recently?" Quentin asked.

"I inherited some money when my grandfather died, and that came at a point in my life where I had no direction. I was bored of my job—I used to work in the restaurant business, on the management side of a big chain—I'd recently broken up with a boyfriend. While I still loved the diversity and culture of the city, I was tired of the traffic and the limited green spaces. I felt as if I needed something new. I'd always had this dream of running a small, independent café or bar, and decided to make it a reality."

"Why did you come to Cornwall?"

"I used to holiday here with my parents when I was a kid. I remembered it as this idyllic place of beaches, ice cream, and pasties."

"So not too far from reality then?" Quentin chuckled, and Jason looked up to see Seb grin.

"I guess not."

"So, tell me about why you decided to make the café queer-friendly. Was that always your intention?"

"No, it wasn't something I planned from the start. Originally it was just going to be a regular café/bar with no particular theme. But one night I was complaining to two good friends of mine about the lack of an LGBT community down here and how lonely and isolated it made me feel sometimes. In my first month here I didn't meet another out gay man. I felt like a freak, and I hadn't felt like that for a long time."

"There are other gay men here." There was a weight to Quentin's tone that made Jason cast his gaze up again. "But most of us are more cautious than we'd be in London perhaps, so we're harder to find."

Seb raised his eyebrows. "We?"

Quentin nodded. "I'm here, and I'm queer too."

"That's good to know." Seb smiled at Quentin, and Jason fought down an unpleasant surge of jealousy.

"Didn't you look on Grindr? You might have felt less alone on there."

"Yeah but I gave up fast. It was all either blank profiles,

guys who were 'discreet'—and that makes me suspect cheating—or guys who were too young for me."

Jason had probably been one of the discreet guys on Grindr who Seb had ignored.

"You're not into younger guys?" Quentin sounded disappointed while Jason was flooded with relief.

"I prefer guys close to my own age," Seb said kindly, then quickly moved on. "So, anyway, that feeling of isolation was the catalyst for Rainbow Place. One of my friends suggested I started a club or society, I jokingly suggested making the café gay, and they convinced me that it was an idea worth considering."

"Aren't you worried about it being a failure? Some people are predicting that it will be impossible for you to make it a financial success." Completely professional again now, Quentin frowned, pen poised on his notepad.

"Of course I'm anxious about how I'll make it work. But any business owner would feel the same. I just have to hope that there will be enough people in the community who support Rainbow Place, and that they will be enough to outweigh the minority who might choose to avoid it. I'm going to make it the best I possibly can. The interior is going to be cosy and welcoming; the menu will be varied and interesting. I've employed chefs who are going to do an amazing job. Our coffee will be fantastic, because I'm a coffee addict and wouldn't settle for anything less. We're going to be offering everything from breakfast, through cakes and cream teas, to evening meals at prices that are fair for the quality of what we're going to provide. I truly believe that if I can make my concept a reality, everyone is going to want to come here." Seb sounded so certain, voice blazing with confidence.

"Except Martin Elliot," Quentin said dryly.

Seb's laugh rang out before he answered. "Well, yes. Maybe not him. But that's probably for the best."

"Right. Thank you so much, Seb. I think I have everything I need, but if I have any queries while I'm writing this up is it okay for me to email you?" Quentin stood, closing his notepad, and putting it in his back pocket.

"Of course."

"And I'll send you the final draft to approve before it goes to print."

"Thanks."

They shook hands at the door.

"It was great to meet you. Best of luck with everything," Quentin said.

"Come to the opening next Saturday," Seb offered. "Have a coffee and cake on the house."

Quentin smiled. "I might take you up on that, thanks."

Once he was gone, Seb came over to Jason. "I think that went well. Hopefully that will be more good publicity. He seemed nice, and definitely supportive."

"Yeah." Jason knew he sounded moody. He was still prickling with residual jealousy, even though Seb had made it clear to Quentin that he wasn't interested. He'd been left unsettled again. It was hard listening to other people supporting Seb when Jason stood by, mute, and useless. Trapped in the closet he'd walled himself into, he felt like an animal in captivity that had outgrown its cage. What once felt like a safe space, now felt like a prison.

Not for much longer, hopefully.

JASON deliberately hung back at the end of the afternoon, sending Will home and finishing up a table that he was sanding ready to varnish while Seb sat working on his laptop nearby.

When Jason was done with the table, he went over to Seb. "Hey. I just wanted to check you're still on for Sunday?" He didn't like how uncertain he sounded, but he needed reassurance. A distance had opened up between them this week. Jason was weighed down with guilt for not supporting Seb, and for keeping their relationship a secret. He wasn't sure whether it was his imagination, but Seb had seemed cooler somehow. There had been fewer eye meets, fewer smiles when nobody was looking.

Seb hesitated, and Jason's heart sank. Perhaps Seb was tired of Jason and his inconsistency. Jason knew his mood ebbed and flowed like the tides in the harbour. One minute he'd be swept along by his feelings for Seb, planning how and when to introduce him to Anna, or to tell Zoe what was going on. But the next he'd retreat, paralysed by the finality of coming out, of saying words he could never take back once he'd given them voice.

"If you don't want to that's fine," Jason managed, throat tight. "I know it's been a stressful week."

"I could probably do with the distraction." Seb shrugged, a small smile making Jason's spirits lift.

"Well I haven't exactly been a source of support this week. But I can definitely try and distract you." Jason moved behind Seb and put his hands on his shoulders. He squeezed, feeling the tension in Seb's muscles.

"Oh God that's good."

Jason massaged him, digging his thumbs in and moving them in circles, seeking out the places that felt tight. Seb let his head drop forward, a flower too heavy for its stem, and silence filled the space around them for a few minutes.

Finally, Seb said, "That was amazing. Thank you." He

tilted his face back and instinctively Jason leaned forward and pressed a kiss to his lips. "I wish it was Sunday already."

"Me too," Jason said.

"Let's make it worth the wait."

WHEN JASON RANG SEB'S door on Sunday night, his heart was pounding as though he'd sprinted there. He'd made a decision earlier, and had spent the rest of the day in a state of nervous anticipation, hoping that Seb would agree to what he was about to suggest.

Seb greeted him with a bright smile and a warm kiss after he'd ushered Jason inside.

"How are you?"

"Good. You?" Jason's voice came out sounding weird—kind of strangled.

Frowning slightly, Seb studied him. "Are you okay?"

"I'm a bit nervous," Jason admitted.

"Why?"

Jason took a shaky breath. "Because I was going to ask you if you'd top me tonight."

Seb's eyebrows flew up. "Really?"

Feeling his cheeks heat, Jason held his gaze and nodded.

"And are you?" Seb asked.

Confused, Jason's brain stalled. "Am I what?"

"Are you going to ask me?" Seb's lips lifted in a teasing smile.

Jason rolled his eyes, his tension easing. "Yes. This is me asking you. Stop taking the piss."

Seb's laughter, and the way he wrapped his arms around Jason before kissing him soundly drove away any last doubts Jason had. He wanted this. Seb drew away, just far enough to murmur, "This is me saying yes," before pressing their lips together again.

Up in Seb's bedroom, they undressed each other between slow, sensual kisses. Once they were both naked, Seb pushed Jason down onto the bed and knelt between his spread legs to blow him for a while. Nervous about what was coming, Jason found it hard to focus. Seb's mouth felt good, but anxiety kept him tense and too much in his head to enjoy the pleasurable sensations in his body. He guided Seb's head away and Seb met his gaze.

"Can we... you... get on with it?"

Seb's lips quirked in amusement. "If you like."

"I want to get it over with," Jason confessed. "I know that sounds awful, but I'm anxious and over-thinking everything, and I just want to get past this part."

"I can understand that." Seb toyed idly with Jason's dick that had deflated in a fit of nerves and embarrassment. "And, Jason, if you don't like it when we try, then we can just stop. This isn't some sort of endurance test or trial you have to go through."

"I know." Jason was grateful for that reminder. This is why he trusted Seb; there was no pressure on Jason to do anything. It was all up to him.

Seb stretched over to the drawer by the bed and got out lube and a condom, leaving them on the bed within easy reach. Then he settled back between Jason's legs and reached behind Jason's balls to press a finger into his crack. Jason bent his knees and tilted his hips up in invitation. He wasn't afraid of Seb's finger; he'd put his own in there a few times out of curiosity so he knew he could take it. Seb rubbed lightly over Jason's hole. His gaze, focused on Jason's face, made Jason feel too exposed so he closed his eyes, trying to stop thinking and just feel.

There was a loss of sensation as Seb took his finger away, but then he brought it back wet with spit and pressed a little harder. Jason tensed, and then forced himself to relax, letting Seb push inside. It felt weird, different to his own finger, but he'd always done it with lube. There was more pressure and stretch, and as Seb twisted it around Jason's breath caught.

"How does that feel?" Seb asked.

"Good.... I think." Jason dared to open his eyes and their gazes locked. He'd never felt so vulnerable as he did now, naked with Seb's finger inside him, curling and pushing and—

"Oh!" Jason gasped at a burst of pleasure so deep it made his toes curl.

"Better?" Seb grinned, doing whatever it was again.

"Fuck yes." Reaching down to touch his cock, Jason found he was hard again. He stroked it lightly, pinned between the delicious sensations in his dick and arse.

"I'm going to add some lube into the equation."

Jason waited impatiently, empty and craving more while Seb lubed up his fingers. This time it felt tighter, a stretching sensation that Jason wasn't sure he liked. "Is that two?"

"Yes. Does it feel okay?"

"I think so." Forcing himself to breathe steadily, Jason waited a moment, giving it a chance. If he couldn't take two fingers he wouldn't cope with Seb's cock. As Seb gently moved them inside him, the discomfort eased and pleasure rolled in to replace it. "Yeah," he said, relieved. "Yeah, it's good."

"Let me suck your dick again while I do it." Seb leaned down and took Jason in his mouth. With wet heat surrounding his cock and Seb's fingers rubbing him on the inside, Jason was soon blissfully lost in a haze of arousal. Too turned on to feel self-conscious anymore he moaned, lifting his hips to meet the suction on his dick, his muscles squeezing around Seb's fingers as he did so. He lost track of time in the slow build of pleasure, and almost forgot what was coming next until Seb finally drew away and asked, "You ready to try my cock?"

Their eyes met.

"Yes." No hesitation, no fear. Only desire.

Seb smiled and let his fingers slip free. "Jerk yourself off while I put the condom on."

Jason obeyed, although there was no need. Hard and leaking, just watching Seb getting himself ready was enough to keep Jason on the edge.

"Do you want to roll over, or stay on your back?"

"Like this." Jason wanted to see Seb's face. "If that's okay with you?"

"Whatever you want." Seb moved into position, his cock jutting out. "Hold your knees back."

A brief rush of self-consciousness returned as Jason held himself open. But the blunt pressure of Seb's cock sliding over his hole soon distracted him. He held his breath, poised on a knife-edge of anticipation.

"Bollocks!" Seb hissed as his cock slipped, missing its goal. "Sorry." He frowned, guiding it more carefully this time. "There... oh *fuck*." He met Jason's gaze, jaw slack with pleasure as he pushed slowly inside.

Jason tensed, bracing himself for discomfort, but when he only felt glorious, cock-stiffening fullness and pressure he let out his breath in a sigh of relief. "Oh God, that feels incredible."

"Yeah?" Seb smiled, withdrawing a little then pushing in again, even deeper this time. He nudged against what

Jason assumed must be his prostate because damn, it felt great.

"Yeah."

Seb lowered himself down and kissed Jason while he started to fuck him in earnest. It was a little frantic, a messy slide of lips and tongues and breathless gasps and moans. Jason's cock was trapped between them, rubbing against their stomachs. The pleasure started to build, swelling, and expanding. He lifted his hips to meet Seb's thrusts, groaning in frustration when the friction on his cock wasn't quite enough. He got a hand between them and started to stroke. "Gonna come soon," he muttered against Seb's lips.

Pushing up on his arms again, Seb fucked him even harder. "Yes. Come on. I want to see you shoot while I fuck you." His cheeks were flushed and sweat beaded his brow; his gaze flitted from Jason's face to his cock and back again.

Jason jerked off furiously, the perfect combination of stimulation sending him higher and higher until finally his climax crashed through him, tensing his muscles as he came, splashing hot on his stomach and spilling over his fingers. With Seb inside him, Jason felt his orgasm there too, deep pulses of pleasure as his body tightened around Seb's cock.

Seb's face contorted as he gave a few final desperate thrusts. "I'm coming too." He pressed deep and stilled, a moan escaping as his hips jerked, eyes squeezed shut. When he was done, he opened his eyes. They grinned at each other, still breathless. "Was that okay?" Seb asked.

"More than okay. Wasn't that obvious?"

"It did look as if you were having fun." Seb eased himself out of Jason and pulled the condom off. Then he collapsed with a sigh, arm flung across Jason's chest. "I'm bloody knackered now. One of the reasons I usually bottom is that I'm too lazy to be a good top."

Jason laughed, putting his arm around Seb and kissing him lightly. "Well I won't make you do it all the time. But now I know I like it... I'd definitely like to switch sometimes."

Seb didn't reply immediately. His silence sent a frisson of anxiety through Jason. He went back over what he'd just said. *All the time. Sometimes.* There were a lot of assumptions in those words, about a future they hadn't discussed yet.

Eventually Seb said, "So... you want to carry on with this then? You're happy with things as they are?"

"Yes. I definitely want to carry on seeing you." Jason sidestepped the second half of Seb's question. "Is that okay?"

"Yeah. I suppose so." Seb pushed himself up on one elbow. "But you need to know this isn't an ideal situation for me."

"I know." Jason felt a lurch of guilt. "I'm thinking about making some changes, though, maybe starting to tell people. But I need to do it in my own time."

The serious expression on Seb's face morphed into hopeful excitement. "Seriously? That's brilliant. I mean, no pressure, and of course the timing is up to you." He turned serious again and held Jason's gaze as he said, "But I want you to know that I really like you. I love spending time together, and I think there's the potential for more than just sex, a lot more. So if you feel the same...."

Mixed emotions churned in Jason's guts like a cement mixer. Happiness, hope, fear, guilt. Knowing that Seb wanted more from him was wonderful, but also terrifying because it meant that Jason had to take action. If he was going to get to keep Seb, he couldn't stay hiding in the closet any longer. "I do feel the same," he admitted in a small voice, wishing he sounded happier about it. "But I'm scared."

Seb pulled Jason into his arms, wrapping his smaller body around Jason's with surprising strength. "I know."

Jason was grateful that Seb didn't try to tell him he shouldn't be scared. He didn't try and tell him it would be okay. He just held Jason tight, the reassuring band of his arms helping Jason contain all the fears that were tumbling around in his head.

"Can I stay here tonight?" Jason asked. It wasn't much, but that was something he could give Seb now, and Jason didn't want to sleep alone.

"Of course you can." Seb squeezed him tighter.

THIRTEEN

Having Jason in his bed when he was used to sleeping alone meant that Seb woke several times in the night. He was pulled into consciousness by the shift of the mattress when Jason rolled over, or by the warm press of Jason's body against his. Each time he woke, Seb remembered who was there and smiled.

Lying awake during one of these interludes, hope burned fiercely in Seb's heart. Jason liked him too. He wanted more, and he was going to come out so they could be together. Seb knew it might take a while, but he had to trust Jason and let him do it his way. He sighed, wishing he was a more patient person. But with Jason snoring on his back quietly beside him, Seb knew he could wait if it meant he got to have this every night. He rolled over, putting his arm across Jason's chest and breathing in the scent of him as he drifted back into sleep.

THE SOUND of his ringtone woke Seb just after half-six.

Scrambling for his phone and mentally cursing himself for not putting it on silent, he saw it was Penny calling.

"Hello?" He lay back on his pillow. Jason rolled to face him, blinking sleepily.

"Seb...." Penny was out of breath. "Sorry.... I was out running... when I saw it. It's the café, Seb. Someone's vandalised it. I'm so sorry, but I wanted to tell you as soon as possible so you can start cleaning it up." Her voice cracked. "They've written some horrible homophobic things."

Cold acid rose in Seb's guts. He didn't want to ask for specifics; he'd see for himself soon enough. "Have you reported it to the police?"

That galvanised Jason into movement. He sat up, a concerned frown furrowing his brow.

"Not yet. I phoned you first."

"Okay. Can you do that next?"

"Of course."

"Thanks, Penny. I'll be down there as soon as possible." Seb ended the call.

"What happened?" Jason asked.

"Rainbow Place has been vandalised." Paralysed by shock, Seb forced his leaden limbs to move, getting up and starting to dress. He needed to get down there and see what had been done to it.

"Fuck. How much damage is there?"

"I don't know the details. Are you coming with me?"

Still sitting in bed dressed only in boxers, Jason looked as stunned as Seb. What an awful way to come down to earth after their first night together.

"Yes, of course." Jason got up and began pulling on his clothes.

RAINBOW PLACE   149

PENNY GREETED them on the street corner. She was dressed in running clothes, and her eyes were red. Tears streaked down her cheeks as she hurried towards them, wrapping Seb in a protective hug. "I hope the police catch the fucking wankers who did this. I'm sorry. I wish you didn't have to see it."

"I can take it." Seb disentangled himself from her embrace. Like a patient waiting for a prognosis, he just wanted to know how bad the situation was. Not waiting to see if Jason and Penny were following, he rounded the corner and even from fifty metres away the shocking pink paint was clearly visible. A large cock and balls was the first thing he could see—how original—but as he got closer he could see there were words too. Sprayed on the walls, and on the windows. Anywhere they could find space to write them.

Words that cut deep and spread like poison through his veins:

Filthy fags
Cock jockey
Butt bandit

The front door—which was hanging open, the lock smashed—had been daubed with the words: *AIDS café.*

Seb's stomach rolled with nausea, and he was glad he hadn't had his morning coffee yet; otherwise he'd have promptly lost it all over the pavement. Heart pounding, hands shaking, he pushed the door open.

Inside it was even worse. The freshly painted walls were ruined with more of the same, the bright pink paint spelling out words of hate and homophobia: *fuck off faggot*; *suck my dick*; another drawing of a cock with the words *take it up the arse* underneath it. They'd even sprayed paint on the furniture and the floor, and when Seb checked he found the kitchen had been targeted too with slogans on the cupboards and oven doors, and random squiggles all over the lino floor. It was a hideous mess. Seb couldn't bear to look anymore.

He left the kitchen and went back to meet Penny in the middle of the main room. Her eyes were still wet but her jaw was set in determination. "Bastards," she said. "Useless waste-of-space dickheads."

"Yep." Seb looked past her to find Jason.

He was standing just inside the doorway, staring at the destruction. Pale, his eyes were wide. He looked even more shell-shocked than Seb was.

Brushing past Penny, Seb approached Jason. "You okay?"

"Shouldn't I be asking you that?" Jason replied weakly.

Seb put a hand on Jason's cheek and tried to draw him into a hug, craving the comfort as much as he wanted to offer it. But Jason stiffened and drew away. "Not here," he said quietly.

Hurt lanced through Seb like a needle. Pulling away abruptly, he muttered back, "It's only us and Penny."

"I know, but just... with all this"—Jason gestured at the walls—"I can't, Seb. I'm sorry."

"Okay. Forget it." Seb turned his back on Jason and got his phone out and started snapping pictures. "I'm taking photos of the damage in case I need them for the insurance claim. Penny, did you call the police?"

"Yes. They said someone will be down soon to take a report, and not to start fixing the damage before then."

"Great. So we have to carry on with all that hate smeared on our outside walls where everyone can see it." Seb lifted his chin and squared his shoulders. "Well, maybe that's not such a bad thing. If nothing else, this little display proves that queer people need safe spaces. Maybe Trude can turn it around to our advantage."

"Good point. I like how you're thinking." Penny sounded more cheerful. "Don't let the bastards get you down. This is what Pride is all about. I've already called Trude. She's on her way down now."

"Jason, what can we use to clean it off once the police have been?"

"The interior sections that are plastered can be repainted, but if we can at least get the worst of it off it won't need too many coats to cover it. Paint stripper should work I think, or some other solvent cleaner. But it will be harder getting it off the external walls, and the floors and kitchen units."

"Will it take long? Can we fix this and stay on schedule for opening day on Saturday?" Looking around at the damage it seemed impossible. "I don't know," Jason said. "Not unless we can get some help."

Seb's heart sank into his boots. "Then they win. There has to be a way we can do it."

"I'll go and buy the stuff we'll need to clean it, and more paint. Then we can get started as soon as the police have been." Jason had a little more colour in his cheeks now, but his expression was still grim.

"Okay, thanks."

"See you later then." Jason left with a curt nod, leaving Seb feeling empty and disconnected.

AS JASON STEPPED out into the street, he felt as though the horrible, ugly words were branded on his forehead for everyone to see. He ducked away from a man unloading a delivery van, unable to meet his eyes.

Cock jockey, butt bandit, take it up the arse.

Jason flinched, the memory of Seb fucking him last night tarnished by the crude slurs that were running through his head. Jason had heard homophobic things before, he'd seen them, read them, heard them from his own father as he was growing up, but they'd never felt so personal before. His chest tightened and his gut clenched with panic.

He had to pull himself together. Seb needed him, and Jason had already disappointed him once this morning. He'd seen Seb's hurt but hadn't been able to get past his own reaction to the vandalism to reach out and offer comfort. If Jason couldn't provide emotional support, the very least he could do was give some practical help instead.

Getting out his phone, he called Will.

"Hey," he said gruffly. "Change of plan this morning, we need to start earlier than usual, and pop out to pick up a few things first. Can you be ready to leave in half an hour? I'll pick you up."

"Sure, boss. See you in a bit."

JASON PICKED WILL UP JUST before eight. He hopped into the passenger seat in the van and immediately started scrolling on his phone, seemingly uninterested in where they were going and why. For once, Jason was grateful for Will's uncommunicative nature. He was glad not to have to explain the reason for their mission.

It wasn't till they were at the trade store adding a huge tub of the terracotta paint they'd been using last week that Will questioned him.

"What's this for? I thought we were done with painting."

"We were." Jason pushed the trolley along the aisle to the section of paint strippers and solvents. He selected a few different ones, unsure which would work best on spray paint.

"So?" Will persisted.

"Some wankers vandalised the place last night, spray-painted stuff on the walls. We need this lot to fix it."

"Shit. Seriously?"

"Yes." Jason remembered the ugly words like a punch in the solar plexus. Thankfully Will didn't ask for more details, Jason didn't think he'd be able to describe the damage without giving himself away.

On the drive back to Porthladock, Jason started feeling really odd. Nausea swirled in his stomach, and he realised his heart was pounding although he was sitting still. He couldn't stop thinking about the slogans on the café walls, any attempts to push them out of his head met with failure. They became voices, the hurtful words playing over and over on a loop. He gripped the steering wheel more tightly with sweat-slick hands.

"Boss, you need to wait for the filter!" Will said in alarm, just in time for Jason to realise he'd pulled into oncoming traffic and was about to turn right through a red light.

Slamming his brakes on, Jason muttered, "Fuck!" waving his hand in a vague apology at a driver who'd braked to avoid him, and was sounding his horn loudly. The other driver scowled at him and mouthed something Jason assumed wasn't very complimentary as he accelerated past. "Sorry," he said to Will.

"Are you okay, mate?"

Jason could feel Will's curious gaze on him like a searchlight. He stared at the lights, willing them to change. "I think I'm a bit under the weather. I don't feel great."

"You look like shit, like you're gonna puke or something."

The green filter finally came on, and Jason made the turning. It was only ten minutes back to Porthladock now and Jason needed to get a grip if he was going to get through the day.

He wasn't sure he could do it.

Will inadvertently gave him the perfect excuse. "Maybe you should take the day off. If you're gonna throw up nobody else will want to catch that."

"I suppose." The idea of avoiding Rainbow Place today was appealing.

The idea of avoiding *everything* today was appealing. Jason wanted to hide from the world until he was ready to face it again. He knew it was cowardly, he knew he owed it to Seb to be there alongside him, helping him deal with this. But he really did feel sick. Perhaps he was genuinely coming down with a stomach bug, and if so, it was better to be safe than sorry. He could text Seb and explain. "Yeah, you're probably right. Okay, I'll drop you off with this lot and then I'll head straight home. Hopefully I'll be better tomorrow."

With that decision made, Jason immediately felt lighter, and some of the symptoms he'd been experiencing waned on the last bit of the drive. As he dropped Will off, Seb was outside Rainbow Place talking to a police officer. The paint was still untouched, even brighter now the sun was higher in the sky, and Jason's stomach lurched again.

He parked on the kerb and helped Will unload onto the pavement, then quickly got back into the van. Seb met his gaze for a moment and gave Jason a small smile. Feeling like Judas, Jason did his best to smile back before driving away.

As soon as he got home, he typed a message to Seb:

Feeling sick. I need the day off today. Sorry, I know it's bad timing.

Sitting on the edge of his bed, staring at the words, Jason was swept away by a tidal wave of shame and guilt. He wasn't really sick, he was just scared. Seb needed him today and he was letting him down. But maybe that was a sign that Seb was better off without him.

He pressed send, and then lay down on top of his bedcovers. Still fully clothed, including his work boots, Jason curled into a foetal position and closed his eyes, hoping that sleep might give him a break from feeling like shit.

His phone remained silent.

FOURTEEN

Seb stared in disbelief at the message on his screen. *Seriously?* Today of all days, Jason wasn't going to be here. His finger hovered over the reply field, but he couldn't think what to say.

He went outside to find Will who was already hard at work trying to clean the paint off the exterior walls. "What's the matter with Jason?" he asked, not even trying to make it sound like a casual enquiry.

Will turned in surprise. "Dunno. But he looked rough as fuck earlier, like he was about to puke."

Seb could identify with that. He'd been feeling sick ever since Penny's phone call this morning, but he was still here.

He didn't have a choice.

Will went back to rubbing at the f of *fags* with a cloth. It was fading, but still visible. Seb wondered whether they'd ever be able to remove it completely, or whether it would leave a stain, a permanent reminder of this hurt he'd been dealt by some random stranger or strangers.

Feeling Jason's absence like a double blow, Seb went back inside.

Trude had arrived a little while ago bearing coffee and cake, and Penny was back now after popping home to shower and change. They'd both taken the day off work to help. Good thing too. With Jason off sick, they needed all the help they could get. Penny was already scrubbing at some of the graffiti indoors, and Trude was waiting at a table with her laptop open in front of her.

"Okay, Trude. What's the plan?" Seb sat down and reached for chocolate cake. Fuck the sugar. He was entitled to misery-eat as much as he wanted today, because this was right up there as one of the shittiest days of his life.

"We publicise this, far and wide, make sure everyone knows what's happened."

"Are you sure that's best? I don't want this to be what Rainbow Place is known for." Seb's dreams had been stamped into the ground and pissed on, and he didn't want to broadcast that to the world.

"It will make the local news anyway, but if we get the word out fast then our story will be the one that spreads. That way we control the message. And our message is that this incident proves *exactly* why Rainbow Place is necessary."

Seb nodded, a tiny seedling of new hope rising from trampled earth. "Okay. So what are you thinking?"

"We post photos of the damage on Instagram, share them to Facebook, and tweet them. Then alongside that we write a blog post about it. We share it everywhere and hope that people pick up on it."

"Do we really want to share the photos? Isn't that just publicising the haters?" Seb frowned. He didn't want to give them a platform for their shittiness.

"I don't think so. By sharing them we're making it clear that we aren't ashamed. We're showing people what the

LGBT community have to face, and that it's the bigots and the haters who are shameful. I know it's a risk, because we're relying on support from the public to fall mainly on our side. But I think most people will be sympathetic, and seeing images of the damage will give a stronger emotional response."

"Okay, fine." Seb shrugged. Half the town had already seen the words on the outside of the building anyway, judging by how many people had come to take a look. "Maybe I could contact Quentin and see if he wants to add something to his interview with me about it? He was planning to publish it on Wednesday."

"Good idea. It will be more relevant if this is mentioned. Shall I get started on the photos while you call Quentin? Then we can draft the blog post together."

"Sounds good." Seb got out his phone. When he unlocked it, Jason's message was there on the screen like a smack in the face. Seb knew he should probably reply, but fuck it. He had other shit to deal with today and Jason could wait. He didn't have time to think about what was an appropriate response. *Fuck you, you spineless twat*, probably wouldn't cut it.

"Where's Jason today?" Trude asked. "I haven't seen him. Penny said he was here earlier."

Raising his gaze to meet hers, Seb said, "He texted to say he was feeling sick. He's taking the day off."

Trude's eyebrows shot up. She looked as sceptical as Seb felt, but all she said was, "Oh. That's a shame. Bad timing with all this extra work to do."

"Yes," Seb managed, his voice slightly strained. "It's not the best." British understatement at its finest. "Anyway, we'd better get on. I'll call Quentin now."

BY LUNCHTIME EVERYTHING was live on social media. Photos, captions, hash tags, the blog post. They'd shared everything and had messaged all their local friends to share it too and spread the word. The number of shares was gradually racking up, but Seb and Trude both needed a break from their screens, and Seb needed to get away from Rainbow Place.

"Let's go out and buy some lunch," Trude suggested. "I think we all need a change of scenery."

"Good idea," Penny agreed from where she was up a step ladder, making good progress on erasing the cock and balls. "My arm's knackered from rubbing this stupid dick."

"Well that's not something I ever thought I'd hear a lesbian say," Seb said with a grin.

Trude and Penny collapsed into laughter, and Seb ended up laughing along with them, his mood lifting a little.

"What's so funny?" Will asked, coming in from outside. He mopped his brow. "Damn, it's hot out there today."

"Just Penny commenting on rubbing a dick." Seb grinned.

Will shot a quick glance at Penny who had an arm around Trude. "I didn't realise how it sounded!" she said.

Flushing, Will tore his gaze away. He was still awkward around Penny, the torch he was carrying for her blazing as bright as his cheeks.

"We were thinking of going out to get some lunch," Seb said. "Do you want to come with us?"

"We can't all go." Will gestured at the broken door. "Not till the locksmith's been this afternoon."

"Oh shit. I forgot."

"I don't mind staying here if you bring me back a pasty."

"Okay. Thanks, Will. We won't be long."

They bought pasties from Cardew's, along with cold

drinks, and delivered Will's before heading back out to sit in the sunshine by the harbour for a little while. It was busy with tourists queuing for boat trips, but they managed to find a bench to sit on near Seaview Café.

Seb had just finished eating when Janine came over looking dismayed. "I just saw the photos on Facebook. I'm so sorry, love. Those people don't speak for most of us down here. Is the damage as bad as it looks?"

"It's pretty awful. And the paint is a nightmare to clean off."

"Will you be able to get it done in time?"

"I'm not sure." Seb wasn't hopeful. Now he and Trude had done the PR they'd be joining forces with Will and Penny this afternoon. But Penny and Trude couldn't give up the whole week to help him, and who knew when Jason would be back?

Janine clucked sympathetically. "Well I hope you can sort something out. It's terrible what they did." She glanced over her shoulder. "I'd better get back, there's a queue building up."

"Thanks, Janine," Seb said. "Your support means a lot."

She surprised him by bending down and giving him a hug. She smelt of strong perfume and coffee. "I just wish there was more I could do."

BACK AT RAINBOW PLACE, with nothing else to do but deal with the damage, Trude went outside to help Will, while Seb worked indoors with Penny. Trude had insisted they did it that way around, and Seb accepted gratefully. He'd feel too exposed outside. The street was busy and through the window he could see people stopping to look at the damage. He wondered what they were thinking, and which of them might secretly agree with the slurs.

By mid-afternoon Seb was utterly despondent. Removing the graffiti was slow, painstaking work. It was coming off, but not quickly enough. At the rate they were going it would take days to clean everything. He didn't see how it could be done in time for Saturday. Perhaps they could postpone the opening by a week. It wouldn't be the end of the world.

"Hi, Seb. I'm so sorry about what's happened. Do you need help?" A familiar accented voice made Seb turn to see Luca standing behind him, hands on his hips. He looked around at the damage with a frown. "This is so wrong."

"Gosh, yes. If you can spare some time that would be amazing."

"Time is no problem. I finished my other job ready to start here, so I'm—how you say—all yours if you need me." Luca's grin was bright in his tanned face.

"Well grab a cloth and get stuck in." Seb gestured to a table with various cleaning stuff laid out.

"Let me just make a quick phone call first." Luca disappeared back out to the street where the reception was a little better.

When he returned after a few minutes he got straight to work with no comment.

Seb's arm and hand were aching from scrubbing at the walls and the solvent he was using smelt horrible and made him feel queasy. He tried to lose himself in the tedious task, zoning out made it more bearable. As a result he lost all track of time until he was disturbed by the sound of multiple footsteps and male voices. He turned to see four large, burly men entering the café.

Seb's heart lurched in fear. "Can I help you?" He tried

to sound authoritative, but his voice wobbled. *What the fuck did they want?*

"Drew. Hi!" Luca called out, hurrying over to greet the leader of the group with one of those manly handshakes that Seb had never really got the hang of.

Drew looked around and shook his head grimly. "Fucking hell; it's even worse than it looked on the photos." Finally meeting Seb's gaze, he stepped forward and offered a meaty hand. "Hi, Seb, is it?" Seb nodded. "Luca told me you might need some manpower, so we're here to help."

Blindsided, Seb shook. "Thank you."

"Everything okay in here?" Trude came hurrying in, flanked by Will.

"Yes, it's fine," Penny assured her. "They're here to lend a hand."

"Drew's my neighbour, and he's captain of the local rugby team," Luca explained. "And these are some of his teammates."

"Baz, Wicksy, and Alan." Drew introduced them.

The other men greeted Seb with nods and smiles that made them look way less intimidating than when they'd first trooped in.

"Some of the other lads can come over later if you want to work through the evening. We're the advance party."

"Yes, absolutely." Seb hadn't thought about what time he'd finish tonight, but if he had willing helpers he'd stay all night if he had to. "Thank you," he said again, glancing at Luca, and then back at Drew. "I can't tell you how much this means to me."

"We want to help. We don't put up with homophobic shit on our team and we're not putting up with it in our town either, isn't that right, lads?" There were gruff murmurs of agreement. "Okay. Where do you want us to start?"

"Perhaps two of you could help outside, and the others in here?"

"Sure."

"Would it be okay if I took some photos of you guys and posted them on social media?" Trude asked. "It's good publicity for Rainbow Place, and for your team too."

"Of course." Drew grinned. "Go for it."

WHEN HE HEARD MORE people arriving a little later, Seb was expecting more rugby players. So he was surprised when he turned to see Janine and Andrew. "We heard that you needed volunteers to help, and we're shut for the day now. What do you want us to do?"

"Where did you hear that?"

"It's all over Facebook," Janine replied. "Look." She showed him her phone where there was a photo of Trude, Will, and the two rugby lads working on the outside wall. The original post was one of Trude's but it had been shared by Baz, saying: *Me and some of the lads are helping sort out the mess at Rainbow Place. Come and show the owner that most of us don't put up with this crap in Porthladock. All hands on deck.*

"Well the more the merrier, definitely. Thank you so much."

Next to arrive were the couple that ran the bakery next door, along with one of the girls who worked there, then Laura from the crystal shop. Another group of rugby players turned up a little later.

"Is it okay if we put some music on?" one of them asked. "I brought a portable speaker."

Trude kept taking photos in between cleaning, posting more to social media. She'd started using #allhandsondeck as a hash tag and #HelpRainbowPlace, and some of the people helping started sharing pictures too.

As each new person arrived, Seb kept hoping one of them would be Jason. But it never was. He felt Jason's absence like a hole in his chest, one that was slowly filling with resentment.

Amber, a seventeen-year-old girl with spiky black hair who Seb had employed as a server, showed up with three other teenagers. Amber introduced one of them, Sophia, as her girlfriend, and the others as Hayden and Alex. Sophia was tall for a girl, with striking blue eyes ringed with black eyeliner. She gave Seb a shy smile, but didn't speak. Hayden had bleached blond hair and he was clearly gay from the flirty grin he gave Seb.

Alex was harder to read. His gaze flickered over the walls, and his expression was pinched as he saw the damage. But he smiled shyly when he was introduced. "Thank you," he said quietly. "For making a place like this. We need it."

Emotion tightened Seb's throat, grateful to be reminded why he'd wanted to do this in the first place. "Thank you for coming to help."

IT WASN'T till Seb's stomach growled that he realised it was seven-thirty and he hadn't eaten for hours. With a flash of guilt he realised that was probably the same for half the people here. He stopped and wandered around, checking the numbers off on his fingers. A quick headcount told him there were twenty-two people inside with another four still working outside.

Raising his voice over the music, Seb yelled, "Who's hungry?" It was impossible to tell exactly how many people replied, but there was a definite affirmative. "Okay, I'm going out to get some food for everyone. Back in a bit."

Seb paused outside to check on the progress. The words on the external wall had almost gone now. They were at least faded enough to be hard to read. "You're doing an amazing job. Thank you so much."

"Yeah, it's nearly there now," Will said. "How's it looking inside?"

"Getting there. At this rate we'll be able to start repainting the interior tomorrow." Then Seb added quietly, "Don't feel you have to stay late, Will. You've been here all day." Jason was the one who paid Will's wages; otherwise Seb would have offered him overtime.

"Nah. I'm not quitting now we're winning." Will grinned.

"Well I appreciate it. Thanks."

Seb walked down the street to the Porthladock Fryer, the local chip shop. The smell of salty grease made his mouth water as he stepped inside. He hadn't been in here before, because fish and chips weren't something he normally ate.

There were two people behind the counter, a teenage boy and a man, who greeted Seb with a cheery smile. "Evening, mate. What can I do for you?"

"Hi. Would you be able to cope with a large order—for twenty-six people?"

"Yeah, no problem. But it might take a little while. What do you need?"

Seb scanned the menu on the wall. "Thirteen haddock and thirteen battered sausages please, all with chips." As he hadn't bothered to take orders he hoped people would be happy to mix and match. There was nothing vegetarian on the menu, but at least nobody would starve if there were chips.

"Right, I'll get that order put together for you. It'll be about twenty minutes."

"No worries, I'll come back for it."

"I can get Scott to bring it round to you. You're that bloke from the new café up the street, right?"

"Yes."

"I'll send Scott over with it when it's ready then."

"Great, thanks. How much do I owe you?" Seb got out his wallet ready to pay.

"Nothing, mate. It's on the house. I saw what happened and I'm working, so I can't come and help you out even though I'd like to. But I can feed the people who are."

"But that must be over a hundred quid's worth of food! At least let me pay something," Seb protested.

"No." The man folded his arms and shook his head. "But if you want to do me a favour in return, take a photo of the food and share that online. You're all over social media and I'm no good at that kind of thing, but if you give us a mention it won't hurt our reputation."

"Deal." Seb smiled, touched yet again by the generosity of strangers. "I'll definitely give you a shout out. Thank you so much. What's your name, by the way?"

"Rick." He reached over the counter to offer his hand.

"Seb." They shook. "It's great to meet you. Thanks again."

He stopped at the small supermarket on the way back to buy a few two-litre bottles of Coke and a crate of beer. That should cover all bases, and there was no shortage of tea and coffee if people preferred that.

WHEN THE FOOD arrived they stopped to take a break. As promised, Seb snapped some photos of the fish and chips before they got totally demolished. He shared them with the comment: *Taking a break from fixing the damage at Rainbow Place with top quality sustenance courtesy of the Porthladock Fryer. Yet again, I'm blown away by the kindness of the local community #allhandsondeck #HelpRainbowPlace.* Then he took a few more photos of his helpers as they ate.

They'd pushed a few of the tables together so they could all gather round. The atmosphere was almost party-like, with dance music blaring from a speaker and the sound of conversations and laughter all around. All the food was gone now, but they were still enjoying a well-earned rest before getting back to work.

One of the younger rugby players, Cam, was squeezed in next to Alex. As Seb watched, Cam said something that made Alex grin. Amber and Sophia were chatting away to Janine, and Penny was deep in conversation with Hayden. Laura was practically nose-to-nose with Luca, who looked utterly enchanted by her.

A seed of happiness germinated in Seb's chest, spreading shoots of hope as he realised that even before opening day he'd already realised his dream. A diverse group of people all under one roof, some queer, some straight, brought together and making new friends and connections.

The door opened, and Quentin came in. "Seb!" he greeted him with a hug that Seb returned. "I'm sorry I couldn't get here sooner, it's been a mad day. I've been following your social media though, and this is an amazing story. I definitely want to cover it. Is it okay if I take some photos?"

"Of course."

Quentin clapped his hands and raised his voice to project over the happy hubbub, "Hey, everyone. Can I have your attention for a moment?" It took a moment for the chatter to die down. "I'm here from the local paper—at Seb's request—and I'm going to be reporting on the wonderfully inspiring thing that's happening here this evening. I'll get round and chat to some of you individually later, but would it be possible to get a group photo for the story?" There was a general murmuring of agreement.

"Where do you want us?" Drew took charge.

"Up against this wall." Quentin pointed to a stretch that was still covered in pink smears, but where none of the writing was still legible.

Drew stood and clapped his hands. "Right, come on then, chaps. One row standing at the back with Seb in the middle, and another crouched in front." Seb could see why Drew was the team captain. Everyone responded to his authority and obediently lined themselves up—apart from Alex who hung back.

"You coming?" Cam asked him.

Alex shook his head unhappily and muttered something quietly to Cam, who patted him on the shoulder. "Alex needs to sit out of the photo," he said. "He's not out to his parents, so doesn't want them to see him in the paper in case they put two-and-two together."

"Well I'm not gay either, and I'm gonna be in the photo!" Baz said.

"Yeah, well you have nothing to hide do you? So nothing to worry about." Cam's voice had a sharp edge.

"That's true. Sorry, mate," Baz addressed Alex sheepishly. "I didn't think."

"You never do before opening your mouth." Wicksy nudged Baz, but his grin was teasing.

"Fuck you."

"You wish."

"Cut it out you two," Drew said. "Right, everyone ready?"

Quentin held up his camera and looked through the lens. "You need to squeeze in a bit more for me to get you all in." They huddled close, looping their arms around each other. "Perfect." He took a few shots, and then scrolled back through them. "Yeah I can use these. Thanks, everyone."

"Right, back to work then?" Drew asked Seb.

"Yes please, if you're okay to stay a little longer. And thank you again, all of you. I never expected any of this."

Seb was overwhelmed by the kindness he'd been shown. He was doubly gutted that Jason wasn't here to be part of it because he would have liked Jason to have experienced it. Whatever conflicting emotions Jason was dealing with today had kept him away from something that might have helped him.

As the others got back to work, Seb had a quick check through the photos that had been shared on social media. He wanted to make sure there weren't any identifiable ones of Alex. Fortunately he seemed to have managed to avoid being caught on camera.

He went to find Alex who was helping Cam clean paint off the kitchen floor. "Hey, Alex. Sorry we didn't check before about photos. I should have thought of it. But I've gone through the ones that have been shared online and you aren't in any of them."

"Cheers. I appreciate it," Alex said. "Most people asked before taking pictures, so I ducked out of them." He hesitated for a moment and his cheeks flushed. Then he blurted out, "My dad's Martin Elliot."

"Oh, shit!" Seb didn't know what else to say, but that seemed to cover it.

"Yeah." Alex shrugged with a wry smile. Then he picked up his cloth and carried on cleaning.

Seb couldn't help comparing Alex's courage with Jason's avoidance as he got back to scrubbing a table that was splashed with paint. Jason had a genuine reason to be here. Seb was paying him for fuck's sake. He huffed out a breath, anger rising up from the hurt and resentment that had been building all day. Even if Jason *was* ill, and Seb didn't believe he was, he could have at least got in touch to find out how things were going. He could have texted or called.

It was like he didn't care at all.

FIFTEEN

Jason's head was aching from staring at his phone screen. He scrolled obsessively, like he'd been doing all evening, looking at the photos of the people helping Seb over and over again. Watching as each new comment appeared on the pictures.

I should be there.

Guilt gnawed at his guts. Would he even be welcome if he turned up now? From the Twitter feed he knew they were still hard at work because they were posting regular updates. Maybe Jason should just man up and go down there. But how would Seb respond if he did? He hadn't replied to Jason's text that morning, so Jason took that as a sign that Seb was pissed off with him—and rightly so.

Jason knew he needed to explain his behaviour and make amends, but he didn't want to do that with an audience.

Instead he carried on scrolling and reading. He was happy to see that most of the comments were positive. The support for Rainbow Place had increased exponentially since the rugby team had started posting about it. There were photos on the team Facebook page that had hundreds of likes, and a healthy—mostly positive—debate had sprung from those about homophobia in sport, and in life. The general consensus seemed to be that the vandals were wankers and that the rugby players were awesome for helping out.

Jason studied a photo of a grinning Seb, flanked by eight burly rugby players. Seb looked gorgeous in the picture. His usually perfect hair was rumpled like it was when Jason had been running his hands through it, and his clothes were grubby and covered with pink smudges. The sight of his smile made Jason's heart ache.

Finally, at midnight, there was a tweet from the Rainbow Place account that read: *We're done for tonight, and done-in. The worst of the paint has been removed. Thank you to all the amazing people who helped us. #HelpRainbowPlace #allhandsondeck*. There was a photo with the tweet that showed the interior. The walls were smudged, but the floor was paint-free and most of the furniture looked clean. There was still work to do. The walls needed repainting, and the furniture that had been targeted would need varnishing. But all that could be done in time for Seb's opening day.

Jason opened his messages and stared blankly at his phone. What could he say to Seb that would make Seb want to speak to him? He was afraid that a new message would go unanswered like the last one, and if he called, Seb didn't have to pick up. Maybe it would be better to talk face-to-face.

WHEN JASON RANG on Seb's doorbell, there was no answer. His house was in darkness. Jason rang again, but still nothing. It was possible that Seb had hurried back and gone straight to bed, but unlikely given the timing of the tweet. Feeling foolish, and regretting his impulsive decision to show up uninvited, Jason sat on the step and looked up at the sky. It was clear, and the stars were bright pinpricks. A half-moon bathed the street in silvery light as Jason waited, the seconds ticking by.

He heard the sound of footsteps and quiet conversation before he saw them coming.

"I can't remember the last time I was this tired," Penny said.

"I can. It was after giving birth to Carson," Trude replied.

"I'm so grateful to both of you." Seb's voice made Jason's heart thump harder. "I wouldn't have got through today without you."

They'd emerged from the shadows now, but hadn't noticed Jason. He stood as they approached. "Hi."

Penny gasped, hand on her chest. "Bloody hell, Jason. You made me jump."

Seb stopped short, staring at Jason. It was too dark to read his expression. He didn't say anything.

"Feeling better now?" Trude's tone was laced with sarcasm.

Ignoring her, Jason addressed Seb. "Can we talk?" Seb still didn't speak. "Please, Seb?"

"He's been flat out since seven o'clock this morning. Can't it wait?" Penny asked.

"It's okay, Penny," Seb said. "I'd rather get this over with."

Anxiety clenched Jason's guts.

Seb hugged Penny, then Trude. "Goodnight, and thanks again. Sleep well." Then he broke away and passed Jason to unlock his front door. "You'd better come in." He turned on the hallway light, and Jason followed him inside.

Leading the way into the living room, Seb turned on the overhead light before collapsing on one of the two-seater sofas. Lying on it, he'd left no room for Jason, so Jason took the other one.

"Well?" Seb glared at him. "Am I right in assuming you weren't actually ill today? At first I hoped maybe it was true. But if you were ill, I think you'd have been in touch to find out how things were going for me."

Feeling sick again, Jason admitted, "Yes. I wasn't ill—well not exactly. I did feel awful when I was out with Will, but I think it was more of an anxiety attack than something physical. Then I used it as an excuse to stay away, when I know I should have been there. I'm so sorry, Seb. I want to make it up to you."

"You can't." Seb's expression was weary and there was pain there too. "I needed you today and you let me down. I can't do this anymore, Jason. I'm tired of being a secret, tired of being hurt by your fear."

"But I'm going to fix it," Jason said desperately. "I just need a little more time. I'm going to come out; I'm going to make things right between us."

"Don't come out just to keep me happy. It's too late, Jason. I'm done. If you're going to come out, do it for yourself—not to try to fix something that's already broken."

A hot lump of emotion was lodged in Jason's throat. His eyes prickled, but no tears came. "Can't you give me another chance?"

"I'm running on empty. I have an insane amount of things to organise by Saturday. I don't have the time or energy for any of this. Please, Jason. Can you just leave now?"

"If that's what you want."

"It is."

Feeling as though someone had punched a hole in his chest where his heart used to be, Jason stood. Seb got up too and followed Jason to the door.

"I'll see you tomorrow then," Jason managed. "Assuming you still want me there?"

"We can't do it without you." Seb sounded as though he wished they could. "So yeah. I'll see you tomorrow."

TUESDAY PASSED in a slow dance of awkwardness. Jason and Seb kept their communication to the bare minimum and were painfully polite to each other when talking couldn't be avoided. Apart from that, they stayed away from each other as much as possible.

Thank God there was a huge amount of work to keep Jason occupied, because otherwise he wouldn't have been able to stand the tension. Despite the sterling work the volunteers had done yesterday, there was furniture to re-varnish, and walls to paint, alongside the last few finishing touches they should have been focusing on this week.

As he worked on the mindless, repetitive task of repainting the walls, Jason went over and over their conversation of the night before. When he'd asked Seb for a second chance, he didn't think Seb had ever actually said no. It might have been implied, but he hadn't said that all-important word. Jason clung to this fact like a drowning man clutching at driftwood. Maybe once the dust settled and Seb was less stressed out about the café opening, he'd be more receptive to trying again. Especially if Jason put his money where his mouth was and actually made some changes.

After work, Jason phoned Anna.

"Hi. Is it okay if I come over to see Zoe tonight?"

"Um, yes. That's fine. But why?"

"I want to talk to her." Jason cleared his throat. "I'm going to tell her I'm gay."

"Oh wow! Okay. I didn't see that coming. But that's great, Jason. You know she's going to be totally okay with it, don't you?"

"I suppose so." In theory, Jason knew Zoe was an ally. She'd shared that post on Facebook after all, plus she was his and Anna's daughter and they'd raised her to be accepting of diversity. But there was a big difference between raising your kid to be an ally, and needing them to be *your* ally.

"Try not to worry. It's going to be fine."

JASON TURNED up with a rampaging flock of butterflies in his stomach. Anna let him in, hugged him fiercely, and sent him up to Zoe's room with a whispered, "Good luck. But you don't need it."

When Jason knocked on Zoe's door, she answered with an exasperated, "What?"

"It's Dad. Can I come in?"

"Oh." Her surprise made it evident that she wasn't expecting him. "Yeah, okay."

She was sitting on the bed with her iPad on her knee, one earbud of her headphones pulled out as she looked up at him in surprise. "What are you doing here?"

"I need to talk to you. Can I sit down?"

"Course." She pulled out the other earbud and moved her legs over to make space so he could sit on the edge of her single bed. Studying him carefully, she frowned. "You look really serious, Dad. What's up?"

Jason took a shaky breath. His heart was beating so hard he felt dizzy. Once the words were out, so was he. He'd never be able to take them back.

"I'm gay."

Her eyes widened. "Are you kidding me?"

He shook his head. "No. I wouldn't joke about this, Zoe. It's true."

"Does Mum know?"

"Yes. She's known for a long time."

"What about Granny and Grandad, and Nan and Gramps?"

"None of them know yet. But I'm going to tell them soon." Jason was dreading telling his parents. He couldn't imagine his father would react well. His toxically masculine, homophobic attitude was a big part of what had kept Jason in denial for so long—and then in the closet once he'd admitted his sexuality to himself. Thank God he could do it over the phone rather than face-to-face. It would be September before they visited next and hopefully the dust would have settled a little by then.

Jason would let Anna explain it to her parents. Jason didn't see much of them either, although they were more liberal than his own so would probably be more supportive. "I'm going to tell everyone soon. I don't want it to be a secret anymore."

Zoe was silent for a moment. Her expression was the one she wore when she was trying to make sense of a particularly tricky maths homework.

"Are you okay?" Jason asked, tension holding his shoulders tight. He desperately wanted reassurance from her. To hear that she didn't mind, that she still loved him, that nothing had changed for them as father and daughter. But he was the parent; he was the one who had to be strong.

"Yes," she replied quickly. "Yeah. I'm fine, Dad. Just... surprised. But it's cool."

"Are you worried about your friends knowing?" That was one of Jason's biggest fears. It would be bad enough if he had a negative reaction from people, but if his coming out hurt Zoe he didn't think he could bear it.

"Not at all. My friends won't be mean about it. It's no big deal these days, Dad. Some kids at school have come out as gay or bi, some other kids at school have gay parents, and Mrs Phillips—our PE teacher—is married to a woman. Nobody cares. I think you coming out is a good thing. It helps other people see that it's okay and nothing to be scared of."

Jason snorted. "I'm not sure about that. I'm pretty terrified actually."

"It's going to be fine." Zoe echoed Anna's words from earlier.

The butterflies in Jason's stomach had settled down, and a sense of tentative peace expanded to fill the space where they'd been. He was starting to believe they might be right. "I hope so."

"Do you have a boyfriend?"

The subject change took Jason by surprise. He shook his head, a twist of pain in his heart as he answered, "No. Not really."

"Not really?"

"There was someone, but I messed up and I think it's over."

"How did you mess up?"

"By keeping my secret, I hurt him."

"But it's not going to be a secret anymore. Maybe when he sees that, he'll change his mind."

"Maybe." Jason was still nursing a glimmer of hope, but he wasn't sure coming out would be enough. It was too little, too late.

"You could try some sort of grand gesture like they do in the movies." Zoe's face lit up with enthusiasm. "Sing outside his window, or hire one of those aeroplanes that pulls a banner behind it, or organise a flash mob of dancers or something...."

Jason burst out laughing. "You watch too many romcoms. Real life isn't like that."

"It could be," she insisted. "If people just made the effort."

Still chuckling, Jason shook his head. Yet she'd planted the seed of an idea. He didn't want dancers, and anything involving singing was definitely out. Perhaps Jason could come up with a grand gesture of his own. Even if he didn't win Seb back, at least it would be a way of apologising again and letting Seb know how much Jason cared about him.

"Can I have a hug?" he asked, opening his arms.

Zoe leaned into his embrace. He breathed in the scent of her shampoo and remembered the sweet smell of her head when she'd been a baby.

"I love you, Dad," she said quietly.

"Love you too." As Jason's heart swelled with affection for his daughter, he thought how strange it was that he could feel happy and sad at the same time. The loss of Seb was balanced by Zoe's love and acceptance. That was what life was like, a constant dance along an axis of positivity and negativity. As long as you had enough good things, you could deal with the bad stuff.

By the time he got home that night, Jason had formulated a plan. He was exhausted, not having slept well the night before after leaving Seb's place. But instead of going to bed, he made himself a strong cup of coffee, got out his laptop, and started to type.

THE ONLY OTHER person Jason wanted to tell face-to-face was Will. Having seen Will's behaviour over the last few weeks, he was pretty confident that Will would be supportive. But as they worked so closely together, Jason thought it was only fair to tell Will in person, and he wanted to see his reaction for himself.

The familiar butterflies were back as he braced himself to get the words out. They were on their way back in the van from picking up a couple of new sofas to replace some that had been ruined by the vandals, the fabric irreparably stained. He glanced sideways at Will, who was on his phone as usual, and decided to bite the bullet.

"Will. There's something I want to tell you. I'm gay."

There was no reaction for a few seconds that felt like forever to Jason as he waited, then finally, "Huh? Sorry, boss. I was busy playing *Candy Crush* and I was in the zone. What did you say?"

"For fuck's sake!" Jason gave an exasperated snort of laughter. "I just told you I'm gay." He fixed his gaze on the road, tapping his fingers on the steering wheel while he waited for Will's response now he was actually fucking listening.

"Oh right. Bloody hell."

"Is that a problem for you?"

"Of course not. What do you take me for?" Will's voice was full of outrage. "You know me better than that."

"Yeah, I do. Sorry. I'm just freaking out a bit here." The rush of honesty made Jason feel even more vulnerable.

"No worries, mate. I think you're allowed to freak out a little. But don't do it on my account."

"So we're good?" He finally dared glance at Will again and their eyes met for a fraction of a second before Jason looked back at the road. All he saw was kindness.

"Yeah, course we're good." Will punched him lightly in the arm, and went back to playing *Candy Crush*.

SIXTEEN

Seb regretted his hasty decision in ending things with Jason countless times in the run up to the weekend. He missed him like a persistent ache in his chest. So many times, he nearly went to Jason and offered him the second chance that he'd requested, but self-preservation stopped him. As much as he was hurting now, it would only hurt even more if they started things up again and it went awry. Seb used to have a rule never to get involved with guys who weren't out, and this was exactly why he should have stuck to it.

He'd broken that rule for Jason once. He wasn't going to break it twice.

BY THURSDAY, Rainbow Place was finally looking ready for the big day on Saturday. All the damage had been fixed and they were back on track. Seb took lots of photos for the website, and shared several to social media with the details about the grand opening. They were doing free tea and coffee with cakes all day, and on the lunch menu it would be buy one meal, get one free. The evening menu would be the same price as normal, but with one free drink on the house.

Both Luca and Amelia were due in tomorrow. Luca would be making some practice dishes to familiarise himself with the kitchen, and Amelia would be baking cakes ready for Saturday. Judging by the responses to his photo posts, Seb was optimistic that it was going to be busy.

That afternoon, Quentin dropped by with his camera. He'd delayed publishing the interview with Seb in the wake of the vandalism because he'd prioritised that story instead. They'd agreed to put the interview out a week after opening, and Quentin had come around today to get some photos of Seb in the café.

He greeted Seb with a hug, and then much to Seb's surprise he went over and hugged Jason too. He muttered something Seb didn't catch, before coming back to Seb with a smile. "Okay, what do you want to use as a backdrop? That corner over there with the standard lamp and the bookcases is nice and cosy. Perhaps I can get a shot of you sitting on the sofa with a cup of coffee on the table in front of you?"

Distracted, Seb turned his attention away from Jason who had his back to Seb again anyway. "Um... yes. That sounds fine."

THE OTHER VISITOR to the café on Thursday afternoon was an unexpected, but very welcome one. Sergeant Hardy, the local police officer who had come to take details on Monday morning, came around with the news that they'd arrested two local men in connection with the vandalism.

"They're brothers, local troublemakers, and were already known to us. A neighbour reported one of them after they saw pink paint on their jeans. Once we had that lead, we hauled both of them in for questioning, because where one of them is involved it's usually a good guess that the other one will be too. We got a warrant to search their houses and found plenty of evidence that should guarantee a conviction."

"I'm glad you caught them," Seb said. "What sort of sentence would you expect if they're found guilty?"

"It's hard to say. Given that they've never been convicted of anything before, they'll probably get a fine and some community service. Maybe a suspended sentence at the most."

Seb wasn't sure how to feel about that. While he didn't think they really deserved locking up, it was unsettling that they'd still be free to come and go as they pleased. What if they wanted to cause more trouble? "Okay. Thank you for letting me know, and thanks for taking it so seriously."

"I'm just doing my job," Sergeant Hardy said, and then he added, "And it was serious. That's one of the worst cases of vandalism I've ever seen. It was nasty too. I don't want people getting away with that—not on my watch."

"I'm glad to hear it."

"Well. I'd best be on my way."

"Thanks again, sergeant. And if you're free on Saturday, please come to our opening day. There'll be lunch on the house for you if you can make it."

"I have a day off on Saturday, so I might take you up on that." Sergeant Hardy gave Seb a small salute. "Thanks, Mr Radcliffe. See you soon."

ON FRIDAY MORNING, Seb went down to Rainbow Place even earlier than usual. Amelia had requested access by 7 a.m. to start her baking marathon. Seb was happy to open up early though. He had a million and one things to do before tomorrow, and the sooner he started, the sooner they'd be done.

Once he'd got Amelia settled into the kitchen and had made some coffee for both of them with the shiny new coffee machine, he left her to it and went to sit at one of the tables with his laptop. Looking around while his computer powered up, Seb experienced a rush of pride in his surroundings. Rainbow Place looked wonderful, even better than he'd ever imagined.

The terracotta walls broke up the sections of stonework and wooden beams, and added warmth to the old-fashioned interior. The flagstone floor was carpeted down the central aisle to reduce the risk of people slipping, but under the tables the stones were smooth and spotless. All traces of the paint-damage were gone.

Subtle overhead lighting boosted the natural light that filtered through the windows, and additional lamps would make it cosy in the evenings when it was dark outside. The furniture was a mixture of reclaimed and new, but the new pieces had been distressed to make them fit with the older items. Most of the tables had dining chairs at them, but in two corners, lower coffee tables were surrounded by two-seater sofas.

There were bookcases displaying the old leather-bound books that Seb had collected from junk shops and car boot sales. Potted plants added some greenery, and the walls were decorated with an assortment of photos, paintings, and prints with a nautical theme—also found on Seb's car boot expeditions.

Smiling, Seb took one last look around before turning his focus onto the tasks he needed to complete today.

He was busy scheduling some social media posts for later when Jason arrived. Checking his watch, Seb was surprised to see it was only half past seven. Jason didn't usually start work this early.

"Morning," Seb said, only glancing up briefly before turning back to his laptop. It was strange and awkward trying to be civil to someone he used to share such intimacy with.

"Morning." Jason approached Seb's table. "Can I show you something?"

Looking up again, Seb noticed that Jason was holding a folded-up newspaper in his hand. "What is it?"

Jason unfolded the paper—it was the *Cornwall Gazette* —opened it, and laid it on the table next to Seb's laptop.

The headline read: *My Life in the Closet: Why I Support Rainbow Place*. Scanning down the page, Seb's eyes flew wide as he saw a photo of Jason. He was dressed in his work clothes, standing by the harbour in Porthladock grinning at the camera, but Seb could see anxiety and tension at the edges of his smile. "Shit. What did you do?" he asked Jason.

"I came out," Jason said simply. "And don't worry. I did it for me, but I thought that doing it this way might help you too. So it's my way of trying to make up for the fact that I let you down on Monday. Read it, please."

Seb started to read, heart beating frantically. It was hard for him to make sense of the words when emotion was overwhelming his ability to think.

My name is Jason Dunn. I've lived in and around Porthladock all my life. I'm thirty-three years old, and I'm a builder by trade. I have an ex-wife and a beautiful daughter, and I'm gay.

I've been in the closet for years because I was too afraid to be open about my sexuality.

"Jesus, Jason," Seb whispered. He couldn't believe Jason had done this—come out so publicly after how fearful he'd been.

My fears kept me trapped and lonely, and it was no way to live. I'm sure that being out will have its challenges too, but I'm ready to face them. I owe my newfound freedom to Seb Radcliffe, the owner of Rainbow Place. He was the catalyst who made me want to change things. I admire his courage and conviction, and his drive to create a community where queer people don't have to be lonely and isolated.

We need Rainbow Place because it will change people's lives for the better. It's already changed mine.

By the time Seb finished reading, the words were swimming through his tears. As he looked up at Jason, one escaped and ran down his cheek in a hot trail. Wiping it away, Seb said roughly, "You didn't have to do this."

"I wanted to." Jason's eyes were glittering with tears as well. "You deserved so much better than I managed on Monday. I can't turn back the clock and change how I reacted then, but I was able to do this. I might not manage to convince the haters, but maybe a story like mine will win over some of the people who are on the fence about whether Rainbow Place is a good thing or not. I hope it might."

"I think it will." Seb pushed back his chair and stood. Moving to face Jason, he said gently, "Consider yourself forgiven for Monday. I was angry, and hurt, but I know what fear feels like, and I understand the need to hide from it. What you did... your story in the paper—that was incredibly brave of you. How do you feel now it's out there? Any regrets?"

"No." Jason shook his head firmly. "None at all. I feel

free. And weirdly, I don't feel scared anymore. My biggest fear was of someone discovering my secret, or guessing, or of being outed by someone else. By taking control of it and telling people on my terms, I feel liberated. I know the people I care most about will support me, and as for the rest? Well, I guess it will show me who my friends are."

"Definitely." Seb searched Jason's expression, seeing a softness there that made Seb believe they were finally on the same page. His heart sped up. "So, that second chance you asked for on Monday night. Do you still want one?"

The hope dawning on Jason's face was like a sunbeam lighting up a dark corner. "Yes." He edged closer and took Seb's hands in his. "Yes, please. I really, really do."

"Can we be boyfriends?" Seb let Jason tug him close. Jason's hands found Seb's hips and Seb held onto the breadth of Jason's shoulders.

"Boyfriends, partners.... Whatever you want to call us is fine with me. I want to be part of your life, and have you as part of mine. I want to sleep together and wake up together. I want to be there for you when you need me, and never let you down again."

Brimful of emotions, Seb had to kiss Jason to stop him talking, otherwise he'd have ended up bawling like a baby. They met in a joyful crush of lips, holding each other so tightly that Seb could hardly breathe. But who needed oxygen? He could survive on the blissful swoop of happiness that lifted him on its wings.

Okay no, maybe he couldn't. "You're squashing me," he managed.

"Sorry," Jason chuckled. "I guess I'm so glad to have you back that I don't want to let you get away again."

"I'm not going anywhere." Seb kissed him again, more gently this time. "I'm exactly where I want to be."

SEVENTEEN

The day of the grand opening dawned fresh and clear. Seb woke early, alight with nerves and anticipation. Even the warm presence of Jason in his bed couldn't tempt him to relax a little longer. Instead he leapt up and opened the curtains, happy to see blue sky outside. It felt like a good omen.

"What time is it?" Jason asked, voice slurred and sleepy.

"Half-five. Go back to sleep if you want. I'm too excited, so I'm going to get up and have coffee. I want to be down there by seven anyway. Amelia is coming in early to start prepping things for the breakfast menu.

"Make coffee for me too. I might as well get up now I'm awake."

They drank their coffee at the table in Seb's kitchen. Seb turned his laptop on and went straight to the Facebook event page for the opening. "Wow, over seventy people have said they're coming now, and nearly two hundred have marked it as 'interested.' Let's hope they don't all show up at the same time otherwise I'll have nowhere to put them!"

Jason moved his chair next to Seb's so he could see. "That's great though. Hopefully it will be enough people to keep you busy all day."

"And all evening too. I hope I have enough staff on to cope with it." Frowning, Seb opened his roster. All his new employees would be there at some point today. Half of them in early till after lunch, and the others overlapping with them at lunchtime and working through to the end of the evening. Seb was planning on staying throughout this first day. He'd be running on caffeine and nervous energy by the end of it, but he didn't want to miss a thing.

"Well I can be around all day if you need an extra pair of hands," Jason offered.

"Thank you." Seb kissed his cheek gratefully. "I appreciate it. Hopefully some of the morning crew will stay on for a few extra hours if we need them. I'll just have to see how it goes."

"Anna and Zoe wanted to come down for tea and cake this morning," Jason said. "Is that okay? I'd like you to meet them."

"Today? I'm not sure I'll give the best impression—unless they like headless chickens. But sure, why not? I'll be so focused on making sure everything is going well that I won't have any headspace left to be nervous about meeting your family."

Jason laughed. "They're not too scary, and they're really keen to meet you, and to check out Rainbow Place. I don't think I could keep them away to be honest."

"Bring it on, then." Seb smiled. The fact that Jason wanted to introduce him was a good thing. It showed his commitment, and made Seb feel more secure in this tentative new relationship.

RAINBOW PLACE 191

"HOW DOES IT LOOK?" Seb asked Jason as they stood outside Rainbow Place.

They'd just finished decorating it with rainbow bunting and bunches of multicoloured balloons, along with a banner that read: *Rainbow Place Grand Opening Today 8:30 a.m.—11:30 p.m.* Signs in the window advertised the special deals for opening day.

Free tea or coffee with anything from the breakfast menu
Free tea or coffee with every cake purchased all day
Lunch menu: Buy one, get one free
Free drink of your choice with dinner tonight

"It looks great, bright and cheerful, and definitely eye-catching."

"Good." Seb checked his watch. "Twenty minutes till showtime." His stomach lurched with anxiety. "I'll go and check on Amelia."

In the kitchen, everything seemed to be going smoothly. Amelia was one of those people who somehow managed to be an oasis of calm when everyone else was rushing around frantically.

"It's all under control," she said. "We'll make the breakfasts as and when they're ordered and we've already started prepping things for lunch."

"Brilliant," Seb said. "I don't know how you do it. I get stressed enough cooking for more than four people."

Tom, one of the kitchen assistants, looked up from where he was chopping sweet potatoes and grinned. "Me too."

"Glad it's not just me then."

AT 8:30 A.M. exactly, Seb unlocked and unbolted the

outer door and hooked it open, then he propped open the inner door too, to make the place look welcoming. The street outside was quiet. A couple of people walking past eyed him, and slowed to read the banner, but neither of them stopped.

Slightly deflated, Seb went back inside to where Jason was sitting with a cup of tea.

"No punters yet," he said, stating the obvious.

"Were you expecting people to be queuing outside?" Jason grinned. "Don't worry, they'll show up soon enough. I bet you anything that you'll be rushed off your feet later."

As he spoke, the first customers arrived. Seb laughed as what looked like the entire Porthladock rugby squad trooped through the door. "Be careful what you wish for, eh?"

"Alright, Seb." Drew greeted him with a back-slapping hug. "We thought we'd beat the rush and come for breakfast." The others who Seb knew gave him nods and smiles as they sat down.

Drew's gaze moved to Jason. "Hi," he said. "You're that bloke from the paper, right? Good on you, mate. That took some balls." He shook Jason's hand firmly.

"Thanks," Jason said gruffly, cheeks flushed pink.

"He's also my partner," Seb said proudly, moving a little closer to Jason's side.

"Yeah?" Drew grinned. "Well good on you both then. Right, I'd better sit down and take a look at the menu. I'm starving."

"When you're ready, please order at the bar," Seb said. "Then we'll get your food to you as soon as possible." A quick headcount showed Seb there were eighteen of them in all. "This lot should keep the kitchen staff busy for a while!" He grinned at Jason.

While the rugby players were eating, other people gradually trickled in. A couple of families who looked like tourists ordered breakfasts, a man with a laptop came and sat at a table drinking coffee and working for a while. Seb made a point of greeting all his new customers personally, welcoming them and making sure they were happy with everything.

Amber, and the other server—a young man called Dylan—were kept busy carrying trays of food and drinks, and clearing the tables as the plates were cleaned.

When the rugby lads left it was quiet for a while, but at around ten o'clock a second wave of people began to arrive to take advantage of the free hot drink with cake offer.

Seb approached a group of elderly women who were tucking into cake as they chatted. "Hello, ladies. Thank you for giving Rainbow Place a try. I hope everything is to your satisfaction."

"This Victoria sponge is very good," one of them replied. "Delicious. But it would be even better with a cake fork." She held up the standard fork, which was all the café had to offer.

"I'll make a note of that," Seb assured her. "We take customer feedback very seriously."

"Smashing tea," another one said. "I'm glad you offer Earl Grey."

"Oh look, Marge." Cake-fork lady nudged the woman next to her. "There's that lovely chap who was in the paper." Seb glanced over his shoulder to see Jason standing at the bar taking orders.

"He's very handsome," Marge said. "Brought tears to my eyes what he wrote," she added to Seb. "That's why we're here. We might be old, but we're not old-fashioned. Everyone has the right to love whoever they want."

Seb's chest swelled with emotion. "Thank you. I'm glad you believe that."

"So does he work here then?" cake-fork lady asked, eyeing Jason again.

"No, Pauline, he's a builder, remember? It said in the article."

"He worked on the renovation of the café," Seb explained. "He's just here to help out today.... He's my partner," he added proudly.

"Business partner?" Pauline asked with a frown. "I thought he was a builder."

Marge rolled her eyes. "Not that sort of partner. He means like a boyfriend, don't you, dear?"

Seb had to work hard not to laugh, but he couldn't hold back his smile. "Yes, exactly like a boyfriend."

"Oh. Well isn't that lovely," Pauline said, beaming. "And how nice that he's here to support you today."

"Yes. Yes, it's wonderful. I'm very lucky."

"HELLO, IS JASON AROUND ANYWHERE?" An attractive woman with a dark bob stood next to a girl with long wavy hair who Seb recognised immediately from the photo Jason had shown him.

Seb could clearly see the family resemblance in person. "You must be Anna and Zoe. Hi, I'm Seb." He offered his hand to Anna who shook it with a warm smile.

"Lovely to meet you at last, Seb."

"Hello," Zoe said, studying Seb carefully as he shook her hand too.

"I think Jason's helping out in the kitchen. There was a rush on and we were low on cutlery, but the dishwasher was already running, so he offered to wash some by hand—" Realising he was babbling stuff that wasn't very interesting or relevant because of his nerves, Seb cut himself off. "Anyway. Find yourselves somewhere to sit and I'll fetch him."

Hurrying away to the kitchen, Seb hoped he'd made a reasonable first impression despite his inane chatter.

"Jason, Anna and Zoe just arrived."

Jason turned, up to his elbows in soapy water. "Oh, she was going to text but I must have not heard the alert. Did you already introduce yourself?"

"Yes, then I escaped to find you."

"I'll finish those," Tom offered. "I'm done with chopping for now, until Amelia finds me something else to dice."

"Thanks." Jason relinquished his rubber gloves to Tom, and led the way out of the kitchen with Seb on his heels.

Anna and Zoe both stood to greet him with hugs and kisses.

"Thank you for coming," Jason said.

"I wouldn't have missed it." Anna smiled at him, and then Seb. "I think this is brilliant what you're doing, it's exciting to be here for the launch."

"Thanks," Seb said.

"So I gather you already introduced yourselves?" Jason asked.

"Yes." Anna sat down again. "Do you two have time to join us? Or are you rushed off your feet?"

Seb glanced at Jason who raised his eyebrows in question. "You're the boss. What do you think?"

"I reckon they can manage without us for twenty minutes or so, and I could do with a caffeine boost. So yes please, we'd love to join you."

Jason and Seb took the two remaining seats at the table.

"Do you want cake?" Seb asked. "Or we're still doing the breakfast menu if you want something more substantial."

"Cake for me, please," Anna said. "And I think Zoe's been eyeing up the cake selection too." The glass-fronted cabinet was in view from their table.

"I'd like some of the rainbow cake, please," Zoe said.

The rainbow cake had pride of place in the centre of the display. Six coloured layers were held together by white icing, and multicoloured sprinkles decorated the top.

Anna got up to have a closer look at the selection and came back chuckling. "Tempted though I am by the unicorn poo cookies, I'm going to go with chocolate fudge cake."

"Coffee for you, Anna?" Jason asked, and she nodded. "How about you, Zoe? Tea? Or would you prefer hot chocolate?"

"Hot chocolate, please."

"What would you like?" Seb asked Jason. "I'll go and order them for all of us."

"Rainbow cake and tea, please."

"Can I give you some money for ours?" Anna asked.

"Absolutely not. These are on the house." Seb stood. "Back in a minute."

As he waited in the queue to place their order, he wondered whether they were talking about him. If they were, he hoped it was good.

The rainbow cake was a huge hit with Zoe. "It's so beautiful. Almost too pretty to eat"—she grinned at them—"but not quite, because *cake*." With that she attacked it with her fork and shovelled a huge piece into her mouth. "Mmmmm."

"Good?" Seb raised his eyebrows.

She nodded, chewing. "Amazing," she finally said when she'd swallowed.

Once they'd finished their cake, they sat and chatted for a little while longer. Jason took Seb's hand where it lay on the table and threaded their fingers together as Anna was asking Seb about his plans for Rainbow Place.

Seb noticed Zoe's gaze take in their joined hands and when she caught Seb looking, she gave him a shy smile. Reassured, Seb squeezed Jason's hand a little harder.

Finally, Seb excused himself. "It's been really lovely to meet you both. But I'd better check on the kitchen staff and make sure they're coping, and get round to greet my other customers. I hope I'll see you again soon."

"I'm sure you will," Anna said. "Maybe the two of you would like to come over for dinner once Ben moves in?"

"That would be really nice. Thanks," Jason said.

As Seb stood, Anna stood too. "Hug?" she offered, opening her arms.

Seb moved into her embrace, grateful for her easy acceptance of him as an addition to their extended family.

Zoe hugged him too. "Will you show me how to make that unicorn poo?" she asked. "One of my friends just came out as bi and I want to make some for her."

"I didn't bake them, but I'm sure I can get the recipe for you."

"Brilliant. Thanks."

LUNCHTIME and the afternoon passed in a blur of faces, food orders, and rushing around. Seb was glad Jason stayed to help, because it got so busy they were struggling to keep up even with all his serving and kitchen staff there. The tables were constantly full, with more people waiting to dive in as soon as another group left.

There were familiar faces along with the new. Sergeant Hardy came and took Seb up on his promise of free lunch for him and his son. Janine dropped by for a quick coffee, and Rick from the chip shop brought his wife for tea and cake. Laura arrived on her usual wave of patchouli and hurried over to hug Seb. "I can't stop. I need to get back to the shop, but I just wanted to say congratulations. It looks fantastic in here and I'm thrilled to see it so busy."

Late afternoon, there was a much-needed lull before they started to fill up again in the evening with customers coming to eat, or just to have a drink and check the place out.

They seemed to be attracting a diverse group of people, which Seb was pleased about. From families with young children to pensioners in the daytime, and young adults through to middle-aged people in the evening.

Penny and Trude came for an evening meal, and Seb was thrilled that they weren't the only same-sex couple dining together. A pair of men in their fifties asked for a table for two, and informed Seb that it was their wedding anniversary.

"We drove all the way from Padstow to eat here tonight. We read about it in the paper and it seemed like fate."

"That's wonderful. How many years?"

"Only married for four years, since that's when they finally legalised same-sex marriage. But we've been together for sixteen years now." They smiled at each other, the mutual affection plain to see.

Seb's heart squeezed with wistful envy, although his happiness for them was genuine. "Congratulations."

A small group of the rugby players returned to sample the beer they had on tap. Baz, Alan, and Cam were among them, with a couple of others whose names Seb couldn't remember. They stood at the bar rather than taking up a table, their lively chat punctuated by roars of laughter that came more frequently as they worked their way down their second pints.

Seb instructed one of the servers to bring them some chips on the house. He thought soaking up some of that alcohol might make for a quieter evening.

Later still, Hayden and Alex came in. Seb was on the till taking orders at the time and he greeted them warmly. "Hey, guys. It's great to see you again. How are you?"

"Good thanks." Hayden glanced at the rugby lads to his right and nudged Alex. "Look who's here!"

Alex locked eyes with Cam, who smiled and gave him a little wave. Alex raised his hand in reply, flushed scarlet, and turned his attention to his shoes.

"What can I get you?"

"A pint of cider, please," Hayden said.

"ID?" Seb asked.

Hayden rolled his eyes. "Coke then."

"Same for me please," Alex said.

"Nice try." Grinning, Seb poured their drinks. "How old are you anyway?"

"Seventeen, but not for much longer. I turn eighteen in two weeks, and Alex's birthday is in June too."

"Final year at school then?"

"Yep."

"Shouldn't you be at home revising for your A levels?"

"Don't you start! I get enough of that from my mum." Hayden pushed his blond fringe out of his eyes. He gave Seb a tenner, and Seb handed him the change from their drinks. "Cheers." Then to Alex, "Where do you want to sit?"

Alex shrugged, scanning the room. "I dunno. Oh... those people look like they're leaving, how about there?"

A couple that had been sitting on one of the sofas were getting up and putting on jackets. Hayden hurried over, neatly taking their place before anyone else could grab it. Alex followed more slowly, with a wistful glance over his shoulder at the rugby players.

Seb noticed Cam's gaze light on Alex where he sat with Hayden. Miles away, Cam didn't notice one of his mates addressing him and had to be brought back into the conversation with a nudge. Smiling to himself, Seb folded his arms, leaned on the bar, and looked around at this little world he'd created.

"What are you grinning at?" Jason joined him behind the bar.

"Oh, I'm just feeling pretty pleased with myself."

"So you should be." Sidling close, Jason put an arm around his shoulders. "Look at what you've made."

Penny and Trude were deep in intimate conversation, their ankles tangled under their table. Other assorted couples and groups were eating, drinking, and talking. The hum of contented chatter filled the room alongside the music filtering from the speakers. The older gay couple celebrating their anniversary were finishing their after-dinner coffee. As Seb watched, one of them reached across to take his husband's hand, wedding ring glinting in the light.

"It's their wedding anniversary today," he told Jason. "They've been together sixteen years."

Jason tightened his arm around Seb. "That's lovely." He paused, and then added in a nervous rush, "Maybe that will be us one day."

Happiness filled Seb, buoyant and bubbly, like champagne. "I hope so."

They stood in silence for a little longer, letting the atmosphere of the room flow over them like a balm.

"This place is exactly what I hoped it would be," Seb said.

Jason turned and kissed his cheek, his breath warm as he murmured quietly, "And this is only the beginning."

ABOUT THE AUTHOR

Jay lives just outside Bristol in the West of England. He comes from a family of writers, but always used to believe that the gene for fiction writing had passed him by. He spent years only ever writing emails, articles, or website content.
One day, Jay decided to try and write a short story—just to see if he could—and found it rather addictive. He hasn't stopped writing since.

Jay is transgender and was formerly known as she/her.

www.jaynorthcote.com
Twitter: @Jay_Northcote
Facebook: Jay Northcote Fiction

MORE FROM JAY NORTHCOTE

The Housemates Series

Helping Hand – Housemates #1
Like a Lover – Housemates #2
Practice Makes Perfect – Housemates #3
Watching and Wanting – Housemates #4
Starting from Scratch – Housemates #5
Pretty in Pink – Housemates #6

Novels and Novellas

Nothing Serious
Nothing Special
Nothing Ventured
Not Just Friends
Passing Through
The Little Things
The Dating Game – Owen & Nathan #1

The Marrying Kind – Owen & Nathan #2
The Law of Attraction
Imperfect Harmony
Into You
Cold Feet
What Happens at Christmas
A Family for Christmas
Summer Heat
Tops Down Bottoms Up
The Half Wolf
Secret Santa
Second Chance

Printed in Great Britain
by Amazon